God
&
Sex

God
&
Sex

Vincent Piccone, M.D.

ReadersMagnet, LLC

God & Sex
Copyright © 2022 by Vincent Piccone

Published in the United States of America
ISBN   Paperback: 978-1-959165-38-5
ISBN   eBook: 978-1-959165-39-2

All rights reserved. No part of this publication may be reproduced, stored in a retrieval system or transmitted in any way by any means, electronic, mechanical, photocopy, recording or otherwise without the prior permission of the author except as provided by USA copyright law.

The opinions expressed by the author are not necessarily those of ReadersMagnet, LLC.

ReadersMagnet, LLC
10620 Treena Street, Suite 230 | San Diego, California, 92131 USA
1.619. 354. 2643 | www.readersmagnet.com

Book design copyright © 2022 by ReadersMagnet, LLC. All rights reserved.

Cover design by Kent Gabutin
Interior design by Dorothy Lee

TABLE OF CONTENTS

Introduction 9
True Love 12
Marriage 15
Adultery 18
Divorce 46
Widows 56
Virginity 65
Homosexuality 68
Rape 74
Incest 79
Prostitution 83
Immorality 87

God created mankind in his image; in the image of God he created them; male and female he created them.

Genesis 1:27

So the Lord God cast a deep sleep on the man, and while he was asleep, he took out one of his ribs and closed up its place with flesh. The Lord God the built the rib that he had taken from the man into a woman. When he brought her to the man, the man said; "This one, at last, is bone of my bones and flesh of my flesh; This one shall be called woman,' for out of man this one has been taken." That is why a man leaves his father and mother and clings to his wife, for the two of them shall become one body. The man and his wife were both naked, yet they felt no shame.

Genesis 2:21-25

"I give you a new commandment: love one another. As I have loved you, so should you love one another. This is how all will know that you are my disciples, if you have love for one another."

John 13:34-35

"This is my commandment: love one another as I love you. No one has greater love than this, to lay down one's life for one's friends."

John 15: 12-13

"This I command you: love one another."

John 15:17

If I speak in human and angelic tongues but do not have love, I am a resounding gong or a clashing cymbal. And If I have the gift of prophecy and comprehend all mysteries and all knowledge; If I have all faith so as to move mountains but do not have love, I am nothing. If I give away everything

I own, and if I hand my body over so that I may boast but do not have love, I gain nothing.

Love is patient, love is kind. It is not jealous, [love] is not pompous, it is not inflated, it is not rude, it does not seek its own interest, it is not quick-tempered, it does not brood over injury, it does not rejoice over wrongdoing but rejoices with the truth. It bears all things, believes all things, hopes all things.

Love never fails. If there are prophesies, they will be brought to nothing; if tongues they will cease; if knowledge it will be brought to nothing. For we know partially and we prophesy partially, but when the perfect comes, the partial will pass away. When I was a child, I used to talk as a child, think as a child, reason as a child; when I became a man, I put aside childish things. At present we see indistinctly, as in a mirror, but then face to face. At present I know partially; then I shall know fully, as I am fully known. SO faith, hope, love remain, these three, but the greatest of these is love.

1 Corinthians 13:1-13

INTRODUCTION

The purpose of this book is to offer a biblical view of how God wants marriage and love to be and compare this to how divorce and adultery pervert human love and marriage.

Human sexuality, love, and marriage are all intricately intertwined. The purpose of human sexuality is to produce children and to provide for the next generation of people. Sexual attraction plays a key role in human sexuality. People want to have sex with people they are attracted to and not to have sex with people they are not attracted to. The game becomes more complicated as many people may be attracted to the same person and one person may be and usually is attracted to many people.

Marriage is the foundation of civilization and all societies. It is the building block of stable cultures. Without stable marriage there can be no stable societies. When marriages are stable society flourishes and when marriages are unstable societies languish.

Adultery and divorce are widespread today. It has effected civilization and society negatively. It has caused grave social disorder and upheaval, injured children and adults, led to the propagation of sexually transmitted diseases, and led to the destruction of biblical values in society.

Adultery, divorce, and remarriage are so common today that the sense of sinfulness about these things has been lost. The Ten Commandments include "Thou shall not commit adultery". At one time people were stoned to death for the sin of adultery, as this was the law. It was also taught that people who commit adultery were in danger of hell. Celebrities, politician's and sports figures who routinely marry after divorce, and have sexual relationships with those other than their wives have pulled the wool over people's eyes to make it seem that these are all innocent mistakes or trivial affairs. Nothing could be further from the truth.

Adultery includes when a person who is married has a social and sexual relationship with someone other than their spouse. Adultery is also defined as when a married person divorces their mate and marries another person. Both the person who divorces and the person they marry are guilty of adultery.

The sin of adultery is necessarily against God's order, against marriage, and against society in general. It is a cancer which destroys both the marriage partners, and society in general. The sin of adultery ruins families, children, and eternities.

This book focuses on adultery, divorce, and marriage from a biblical point of view. It takes passages from the bible and expands on them to explain how God thinks about adultery and divorce and why they are so distasteful in his sight. The feast of sexuality is good in God's sight when it involves two people, man and woman, married to each other. It is abhorrent in any other sense to include adultery. A feast of sexuality when shared with a married person and someone other than their spouse is disgraceful and sinful in God's sight.

A high adultery rate and high divorce rate in a country or age is indicative of grave social disorder and precedes social breakdown. Societies cannot remain stable when the pillars of civilization, the family and the marriage, breakdown. High divorce rates and remarriage are in essence bedhopping and wifeswapping. Adultery is associated with higher frequencies of mental disorders and sexually transmitted diseases.

Adulterous remarriage situations cannot be undone nor can the sinful stain of adultery be bleached clean. Hopefully this book will set people straight as to what is acceptable and unacceptable behavior. Adultery has become so entrenched, so popular, so widespread, and so trivialized as to make it almost impossible to change the popular culture. Change however it must or society will dissolve.

Careful choice of marriage partners, return to respect for marriage, respect for the marriage bed, are all necessary to reverse the divorce-adultery culture. Anything short of stoning people must be used to return people to their senses.

TRUE LOVE

Set me as a seal on your heart, as a seal on your arm; For stern as death is love, relentless as the netherworld is devotion; its flames are a blazing fire. Deep waters cannot quench love, nor floods sweep it away. Were one to offer all he owns to purchase love, he would be roundly mocked.
Song of Songs 8:6b-7

Hopefully before a man marries a woman they fall deeply in love with one another and their hearts become set on each other. This is the standard for a successful marriage. When a person marries for position, or wealth, or fame or anything other than true love the marriage is set on rocky ground. True love is resistant against the buffets and vicissitudes of life and will truly last. True loves resists aging and is renewed on a daily basis. As in the book of Tobit in the bible, Sarah and Tobiah were set apart for each other before the world existed. This is the standard for true biblical love.

Love is defined as a warm personal attachment or deep affection for another. It is a warm fondness or liking for another. It is the strong or passionate affection for a person of the opposite sex which constitutes the emotional incentive to conjugal union. Love is also defined as wanting the good for another person. Sexual love binds a man and a woman into "one body". Love should be the basis of all human relationships and is the basis for the institution of marriage.

The human standard for love is best defined in first Corinthians Chapter 13—"If I speak in human and angelic tongues but do not have love, I am a resounding gong or a clashing cymbal. And if I have the gift of prophecy and comprehend all mysteries and all knowledge; if I have all faith so as to move mountains but do not have love, I am nothing. If I give away everything I own, and if I hand my body over so that I may boast but do not have love, I gain nothing. Love is patient, love is kind. It is not jealous, [love] is not pompous, it is not inflated, it is not rude, it does not seek its own interests, it is not quick-tempered, it does not brood over injury, it does not rejoice over wrongdoing but rejoices with the truth. It bears all things, believes all things, hopes all things, endures all things.

Jesus commanded all his disciples three times to love one another and surely this command applies to husband and wife. Jesus meant that women and men remain married and love one another as long as they lived or until one person dies. True love between man and woman in marriage was the standard wished by God for his people. Conjugal love was meant for the creation of children, and the mutual love of husband and wife was meant to be an example for children and as an example for these children of God's love for them.

Happiness of man and wife was found in stable healthy marriages and the prosperity of people was found there. The description of the ideal wife was found in Ecclesiastes 31: 10-31—"When one finds a worthy wife her value is far beyond pearls. Her husband entrusting his heart to her, has an unfailing prize. She brings him good and not evil, all the days of her life. She obtains wool and flax and makes cloth with skillful hands. Like merchant ships, she secures her provisions from afar. She rises while it is still night, and distributes food to her household. She picks out a field to purchase; out of her earnings she plants a vineyard. She is girt with strength, and sturdy are her arms. She enjoys the success of her dealings; at night her lamp is undimmed. She puts her hands to the distaff, and her fingers ply the spindle. She reaches out her hands to the poor, and extends her arms to the needy. She fears not her snow for her household; all her charges are doubly clothed. She makes her own coverlets; fine linen and purple are her clothing. Her husband is prominent at the city gates and he sits with the elders of the land. She makes garments and sells them, and stocks the merchants with belts. She is clothed with strength and dignity, and she laughs at the days to come. She opens her mouth in wisdom, and on her tongue is kindly counsel. She watches the conduct of her household, and eats not her food in idleness. Her children rise up and praise her; her husband, too, extols her: "Many are the women of proven worth, but you have excelled them all." Charm is deceptive and beauty fleeting; the woman who fears the Lord is to be praised. Give her a reward of her labors, and let her works praise her at the city gates.

MARRIAGE

A worthy wife is the crown of her husband, but a disgraceful one is like rot in his bones.
Proverbs 12:4

He who finds a wife finds happiness, it is a favor he receives from the LORD
Proverbs 18:22

Home and possessions are an inheritance from parents, but a prudent wife is from the LORD.
Proverbs 19:14

Dismiss not a sensible wife; a gracious wife is more precious than corals.
Sirach 7:19

Now in regard to the matters about which you wrote: "It is a good thing for a man not to touch a woman," but because of cases of immorality every man should have his own wife, and every woman her own husband. The husband should fulfill his duty towards his wife, and likewise the wife toward her husband. A wife does not have authority over her own body, but rather her husband, and similarly a husband does not have authority over his own body, but rather his wife. Do not deprive each other, except perhaps by mutual consent for a time, to be free for prayer, but then return to one another, so that Satan may not tempt you through your lack of self control. This I say by way of concession, however, not as a command. Indeed, I wish everyone to be as I am, but each has a particular gift from God, one of one kind and one of another. Now to the unmarried and widows, I say: IT is a good thing to remain as they are, as I do, but if they cannot exercise self-control they should marry, for it is better to marry than to be on fire. To the married, however, I give this instruction (not I, but the Lord): A wife should not separate from her husband—and if she does separate she must either remain single or become reconciled to her husband—and a husband should not divorce his wife.

1 Corinthians 7:1-11

This is the will of God, your holiness: that you refrain from immorality, that each of you know how to acquire a wife for himself in holiness and honor, not in lustful passion as the Gentiles who do not know God; not to take advantage of or exploit a brother in this matter, for the Lord is an avenger in all these things, as we told you before and solemnly affirmed. For God did not call us to impurity but to holiness. Therefore, whoever disregards this, disregards not a human being but God, who [also] gives his holy spirit to you.

1 Thessalonians 4:3-8

Many marriages are stressed by illegal drug use, pornography, gambling, alcohol use, obesity, psychological and psychiatric problems and domestic violence. People often divorce to escape mates who suffer such afflictions. If they remarry it is often into similar or same problems. Some people fail to seek counsel from psychiatrists and psychologists, and others who do seek such help fail to be helped. It is doubtful that these problems were not present before marriage and these people sometimes married the problem. Should the marriage bond be called to supervene these problems. Well what does divorce accomplish and what does remarriage accomplish? All it does is take broken people and put them on the market again. The problems which underlie the broken marriage worsen and are never fixed. Perhaps a married couple, the healthier partner at least, should throw out the extra food or not buy so much, tear up the pornography, take control of the bank accounts and control the finances in the case of compulsive gambling, put the effected partner into drug rehabilitation or jail, pour the alcohol down the sink, or make sure their mentally ill spouse take their medication and go the psychiatric unit, and be put in jail for domestic violence.

ADULTERY

David and Bathsheba

King David after his afternoon sleep looked over the city from the palace and saw a naked woman bathing on a roof. She was very beautiful. King David inquired and found that her name was Bathsheba. She was married. King David called the woman to his residence and had sex with her. She got pregnant.

King David, assigned Bathsheba's husband, Uriah, who was in the army of King David, to the hottest area of battle in a war king David was engaged in. Bathsheba's husband died in battle as was King David's intent. King David took Bathsheba as his wife.

Nathan, an advisor to King David, heard of the affair and about the death of the husband of Bathsheba. He foretold that Bathsheba's unborn child would die and that trouble would never leave David's house in the future.

He story of David and Bathsheba illustrates several truth's about adultery.

The first point is that the sin of adultery always hurts more than one person. In the case of David and Bathsheba, it caused David and the house of David to be cursed in the future, Bathsheba's child died, Uriah was killed, and Bathsheba had to live with the death of her husband and the loss of a child. Significantly it also effects our relationship with God. The adulterous behavior always effects the married partner of those involved in the affair. There is disappointment, mistrust, and a sense of betrayal.

Adultery can also result in children from the illicit relationship. The children are illegitimate and are stigmatized for the rest of their lives. Adultery can also result in abortion, the destruction of human life.

Adultery also effects how other people view the two adulterers. In ancient times these people were stoned to death. In more recent times these people were stigmatized as people who did not respect marriage vows or the marriage bed.

Significantly adultery effects our relationship with God and his relationship with us. People harden their hearts when they sin against God. Sirach Chapter 23 versus 18-26 is telling; "And, the man who dishonors his marriage bed and says to himself, "Who can see me? Darkness surrounds me , walls hide me ; no one sees me; why should I fear to sin? Of the most high he is not mindful, fearing only the eyes of men; He does not understand that the eyes of the Lord, ten thousand times brighter than the sun, Observe every step a man takes and peer into hidden corners. He who knows all things before they exist still knows them all after they are made. Such a man will be punished in the streets of the city; and when he least suspects it, he will be apprehended. So also with the woman who is unfaithful to her husband and offers as heir her son by a stranger. First, she has disobeyed the law of the Most High; secondly she has wronged her husband; Third in her wanton adultery she has borne children by another man. Such a woman will be dragged before the assembly, and her punishment will extend to her children; Her children will not take root; her branches will not bring forth fruit. She will leave an accursed memory; her disgrace will never be blotted out.

<u>The Ordeal</u>

The Lord said to Moses, Speak to the Israelites and tell them: If a man's wife goes astray and becomes unfaithful to him by having intercourse with another man though her husband has not sufficient evidence of the fact, so that her impurity remains unproved for lack of a witness who might have caught her in the act; or if a man is overcome by a feeling of jealousy that makes him suspect his wife whether she was actually impure or not: he shall bring his wife to the priest and shall take along as an offering for her a tenth of an ephah of barley meal. However he shall not pour oil on it nor put frankincense over it, since it is a cereal offering for an appeal in a question of guilt.

" The priest shall first have the woman come forward and stand before the Lord. In an earthen vessel he shall meanwhile put some holy water, as well as some dust that he has taken from the floor of the Dwelling. Then, as the woman stands before the Lord, the priest shall uncover her head and place in her hands the cereal offering of her appeal, that is the cereal offering of jealousy, while he himself shall hold the bitter water that brings a curse. Then, he shall adjure the woman, saying to her, " If no other man has had intercourse with you, and you have not gone astray by impurity while under the authority of your husband, be immune to the curse brought by this bitter water. But if you have gone astray while under the authority of your husband and have acted impurely by letting a man other than your husband have intercourse with you—so shall the priest adjure the woman with this oath of imprecation—' may the lord make you an example of malediction and imprecation among your people by causing your thighs to waste away and your belly to swell. May this water, then, that brings a curse, enter your body to make your body swell and your thighs waste away! And the woman shall say , 'Amen, amen!' The priest shall put these imprecations in writing and shall then wash then off into the bitter water, which he is to have the woman drink, so that it may go into her with all its bitter curse. But first he shall then take the cereal offering of jealousy from the woman's hand and having waved this offering before the Lord, shall pout it near the altar, ., where he shall take a handful of the cereal offering as its token offering and burn it on the altar. Only then shall he have the woman drink the water. Once she has done so, if she has been impure and unfaithful to her husband, this bitter water that brings a curse will go into her, and her belly will swell and her thighs waste away, so that she will become an example of imprecation among her people. If, however, the woman has not defiled herself, but is still pure, she will be immune and will still be able to bear children.

This, then is the law for jealousy: When a woman goes astray while under the authority of her husband and acts impurely, or when such a feeling of jealousy comes over a man that he become suspicious of his wife, he shall have her stand before the Lord, and the priest shall apply this law in full to her. The man shall be free from guilt, but the woman shall bear such guilt as she might have.

Numbers 5:11-31

The bitter water would adversely affect the health of a woman who was guilty of adultery but leave her unscathed if she were innocent and her husband merely jealous. Numbers deals with when a woman is merely suspected of adultery and there is no proof. Presumably the woman would be stoned to death if she were actually caught in the act of adultery. The book of numbers and the requirement to stone a woman when she was caught in the act of adultery shows just how harsh the law was when it came to adulterers. The law was meant to protect marriage and the family and to put the fear of God in those who would break the commandment you shall not commit adultery.

Perhaps the bitter water should be returned to current life. If women knew they would be poisoned by the bitter water if they committed adultery they might think twice before they did. Again, if people knew they would be stoned to death if they committed adultery perhaps they would not break this command. It is difficult to balance the need for family stability and adultery free marriage from the difficult choice to stone people if they are found to commit adultery. On the one hand if marriage becomes so broken down an institution because people cheat on one another that families no longer survive and children are injured that is one thing. On the other hand you may have a lot of dead people on your hands if the practice is widespread.

No Heaven

Do you not know that the unjust will not inherit the kingdom of God? Do not be deceived; neither fornicators nor idolaters nor adulterers nor boy prostitutes nor sodomites nor thieves nor the greedy nor drunkards nor

slanderers nor robbers will inherit the kingdom of God. That is what some of you used to be; but now you have had yourselves washed, you were sanctified, you were e justified in the name of the lord Jesus Christ in the Spirit of our God.

1 Corinthians 6:9-11

This new testament passage makes it clear that adulterers who do not change their ways will not enter into the kingdom of God—Heaven. People in marriages who have sexual relationships with people outside the marriage and continue to do this will go to hell. This also applies to people outside of a marriage who have a sexual relationship with married people. With the revelations of Jesus people who divorce and remarry are also at risk of hell and people who marry divorced people are also at risk of hell.

Thus when you read, or hear, or see of people who have forsaken their marriage vows from one to another look at them with pity for their eternity will be terrible. So to those who enter with a sexual relationship to a married person who is not their mate. This information is not presented in books except the bible, on television, radio, or movies. How many people are mislead by the media into thoughts that adultery is acceptable. In an era of sexual promiscuity and licentious behavior there is no notation or posting that eternal souls are at risk..

People who go to church and marry there take vows that they will love each other till death do they part and even afterwards. They also take vows for better or worse, for richer or poorer, in health and in sickness. These vows before God are sacred. When the marriage bond is broken by adultery this is not taken lightly by God. The marriage at city hall is no less supposed to be honored by those who enter into that marriage.

Marriage is supposed to outlast the era of disposable people. Married couple are not to forsake their partners when something supposedly better comes around. There marriage vows extend for as long as they live.

Marriage then is something not to be entered into lightly but with forethought and reflection. A period of time in courtship is necessary to see if the marriage will endure and if the couple's faults and gifts are compatible for the longterm.

Jesus's revelation about marriage and divorce extend the concept of adultery to those who divorce and remarry. Even though this might not be accepted as truth by today's society it is in fact the truth. People who commit adultery gravely jeopardize their souls and their eternity. It is also written what God has joined let no man separate. People who seek to destroy marriages to their own benefit or out of jealousy also threaten their own souls.

Lead us not into temptation But deliver us from evil

There are two stories from the bible that tell us how to deal with potentially adulterous situations. They are the story of Joseph from the book of Genesis and the story of Susanna from the book of Daniel.

When Joseph was taken down to Egypt, a certain Egyptian (Potiphar, a courtier of Pharaoh and his chief steward) bought him from the Ishmaelites who had brought him there. But since the Lord was with him, Joseph got on very well and was assigned to the household of his Egyptian master. When his master saw that the Lord was with him and brought him success in whatever he did, he took a personal liking to Joseph and made him his personal attendant; he put him in charge of his household and entrusted him all his possessions. From the moment that he put him in charge of all his possessions, the LORD blessed the Egyptian's house for Joseph's sake; in fact, the LORD's blessing was on everything he owned, both inside the house and out. Having left everything he owned in Joseph's charge, he gave no thought, with Joseph there, to anything but the food he ate.

Now Joseph was strikingly handsome in countenance and body. After a time, his master's wife began to look fondly at him and said, "Lie with me." But he refused. "As long as I am here," he told her, "my master does not concern himself with anything in the house, but has entrusted to me all he owns. He wields no more authority in this house than I do, and he has withheld from me nothing but yourself since you are his wife. How, then, could I commit so great a wrong and thus stand condemned before God?" Although she tried to entice him day after day, he would not agree to lie beside her, or even stay near her.

One such day, when Joseph came into the house to do his work, and none of the household servants were there in the house, she laid hold of him by his cloak, saying, "Lie with me!" But leaving the cloak in her hand, he got away from her and ran outside. When she saw that he had left his cloak in her hand as he fled outside, she screamed for her household servants and told them, "Look! My husband has brought in a Hebrew slave to make sport of us! He came in here to lie with me, but I cried out as loud as I could. When he heard me scream for help, he left his cloak beside me and ran away outside."

She kept the cloak with her until his master came home. Then she told him the same story: "The Hebrew slave whom you brought here broke in on me, and made sport of me. But when I screamed for help, he left his cloak beside me and fled outside." As soon as the master heard his wife's story about how his slave had treated her, he became enraged. He seized Joseph and threw him into the jail where the royal prisoner's were confined.

But even while he was in prison, the LORD remained with Joseph; he showed him kindness by making the chief jailer well-disposed towards him. The chief jailer put Joseph in charge of all the prisoner's in the jail, and everything that had to be done there was done under his management. The chief jailer did not concern himself with anything at all that was in Joseph's charge, since the LORD was with him and brought success to all he did.

Genesis 39:1-23

In Babylon there lived a man named Joakim, who married a very beautiful and God fearing woman, Susanna, the daughter of Hilkiah; her pious parents had trained their daughter according to the law of Moses. Joakim was very rich; he had a garden near his house, and the Jews had recourse to him often because he was the most respected of them all.

That year, two elders of the people were appointed judges of whom the Lord said, "Wickedness has come out of Babylon: from the elders who were to govern the people as judges." These men, to whom all brought their cases, frequented the house of Joakim. When the people left at noon, Susanna used to enter her husband's garden for a walk. When the old men saw her enter every day for her walk, they began to lust for her. They suppressed their consciences; they would not allow their eyes to look to heaven, and did not keep in mind just judgments. Though both were enamored of her, they did not tell each other their trouble, for they were ashamed to reveal their lustful desire to have her. Day by day they watched eagerly for her. One day they said to each other, "let us be off for home; it is time for lunch." So they went out and parted; but they both turned back, and when they met again, they asked each other the reason. They admitted their lust, and they agreed to look for an occasion when they could meet her alone.

One day, while they were waiting for the right moment, she entered the garden as usual, with two maids only. She decided to bathe, for the weather was warm. Nobody else was there except the two elders, who had hidden themselves and were watching her. "Bring me oil and soap," she said to the maids, "and shut the garden doors while I bathe." They did as she said; they shut the garden doors and left by the side gate to fetch what she had ordered, unaware that the elders were hidden inside.

A soon as the maids had left, the two old men got up and hurried to her. "Look," they said, " the garden doors are shut, and no one can see us; give in to our desire, and lie with us. If you refuse, we will testify against you that you dismissed your maids because a young man was here with you."

"I am completely trapped," Susanna groaned. " If I yield, it will be my death; if I refuse, I cannot escape you power. Yet it is better for me to fall into your power without guilt than to sin before the Lord." Then Susanna shrieked, and the old men also shouted at her, as one of them ran to open the garden doors. When the people in the house heard the cries from the garden, they rushed in by the side gate to see what had happened to her. At the accusations by the old men, the servants felt very much ashamed, for never had any such thing been said about Susanna.

When the people came to her husband Joakim the next day, the two wicked elders also came, fully determined to put Susanna to death. Before all the people they ordered: "Send for Susanna, the daughter of Hilkiah, the wife of Joakim." When she was sent for, she came with her parents, children and all her relatives. Susanna, very delicate and beautiful, was veiled; but those wicked men ordered her to uncover her face so as to sate themselves with her beauty. All her relatives and the onlookers were weeping.

In the midst of the people the two elders rose up and laid their hands on her head. Through her tears she looked up to heave, for she trusted in the Lord wholeheartedly. The elders made this accusation: "As we were walking in the garden alone, this woman entered with two girls and shut the doors of the garden, dismissing the girls. A young man, who was hidden there, came and lay with her. When we, in a corner of the garden, saw this crime, we ran toward them. We saw them lying together, but the man we could not hold, because he was stronger than we; he opened to doors and ran off. Then we seized this one and asked who the young man was, but she refused to tell us. We testify to this." The assembly believed them, since they were elders and judges of the people, and they condemned her to death.

But Susanna cried aloud: " O eternal God, you know what is hidden and are aware of all things before they come to be: you know that they have testified falsely against me. Here I am about to die, though I have done of the things with which these wicked men have charged me."

The Lord heard her prayer. As she was being led to execution, God stirred up the spirit of a young man named Daniel, and he cried aloud: "I will have no part in the death of this woman." All the people turned and asked him, " What is this you are saying?" He stood in their midst and continued, " Are you such fools, O Israelites! To condemn a woman of Israel without examination and without clear evidence? Return to court, for they have testified falsely against her."

Then all the people returned in haste. To Daniel the elders said, " Come sit with us and inform us, since God has given you the prestige of old age. But he replied, "Separate these two far from one another that I may examine them."

After they were separated one from another, he called one of them and said: "How you have grown evil with age! Now have your past sins come to term: passing unjust sentences, condemning the innocent, and freeing the guilty, although the Lord says, 'The innocent and the just you shall not put to death.' Now then if you were a witness, tell me under which tree you have seen them together." Under a mastic tree, he answered. Your fine lie has cost you your head," said Daniel: "for the angel of the Lord shall receive the sentence from him and split him in two." Putting him to one side, he ordered the other one, to be brought. "Offspring of Canaan, not of Judah," Daniel said to him, beauty has seduced you, lust has subverted your conscience. This is how you acted with the daughters of Israel, and in their fear they yielded to you; but a daughter of Judah did not tolerate your wickedness. Now then, tell me under what tree you surprised them together." "Under an oak," he said. "Your fine lie has cost you also your head," said Daniel; "for the angel of God waits with a sword to cut you in two so as to make an end of you both."

The whole assembly cried aloud, blessing God who saves those who hope in him. They rose up against the two elders, for by their own words Daniel had convicted them of perjury. According to the law of Moses, they inflicted on them the penalty they had plotted to impose on their neighbor: they put them to death. Thus was innocent blood spared that day.

Hilkiah, and his wife praised God for their daughter Susanna, as did Joachim her husband and all her relatives, because she was found innocent of any shameful deed.

Daniel 13 1-64

Fatal Attraction

"Avert your eyes from a comely woman; gaze not upon the beauty of another's wife- Through woman's beauty many perish, for lust for it burns like fire. With a married woman dine not, recline not at table to drink by her side, Lest your heart be drawn to her and you go down in blood to the grave."

Sirach 9:8-9

Attraction can be fatal! Whether a man is married, single, or divorced if he begins to consort with a woman who is married to another man, both his body and soul are in trouble. What man is not attracted to a beautiful woman?

Yet if this is another man's wife it can cause trouble to even look at her

The trick to beat the temptation of another man's wife is to avert your glance from her and not directly look or stare at her. It is also important to dine with another's wife especially if she is attractive.

The Commandment

"You shall not commit adultery"
Exodus 20:14

"You shall not have carnal relations with your neighbors wife, defiling yourself with her"
Leviticus 18:20

"If a man is discovered having relations with a woman who is married to another, both the man and the woman with whom she has had relations shall die. Thus shall you purge the evil from your midst."
Deuteronomy 22:22

The above laws made it quite clear that when a married man or woman had relations with someone other than their spouse that they committed adultery. It also made clear that when anyone whether they were married, divorced, or single and never married had sexual relations with some one who was married then that person was guilty of adultery. Adultery was prohibited by the ten commandments. Adultery was punishable by death in the ancient world. Both the married person and the other person whether divorces, married, or single were to be put to death. There was no double penalty for a married man or woman having relations with another persons wife or husband although there probably should be.

The law was meant to protect the institution of marriage, to insure offspring were of one couple only, and to prevent the transmission of sexually transmitted diseases. The law was also meant to make sure that the family was holy in the presence of God.

The command against adultery was so important that it was included with the ten primary ones so that it was absolutely followed by the people. To some extent the command was repeated in the last commandment that you shall not covet thy neighbors wife.

Caught

Then each went to his own house, while Jesus went to the mount of Olives. But early in the morning he arrived again in the temple area, and all the people started coming to him, and he sat down and taught them. Then the scribes and the Pharisees brought a woman who had been caught in adultery and made her stand in the middle. They said to him, "Teacher, this woman was caught in the very act of committing adultery. Now in the law, Moses commanded us to stone such women. So what do you say?" They said this to test him, so that they could have some charge against him. Jesus bent down and began to write on the ground with his finger. But when they continued asking him, he straightened up and said to them, " Let the one among you who is without sin be the first to throw a stone at her." Again he bent down and wrote on the ground. And in response, they went away, one by one, beginning with the elders. So he was left alone with the woman before him. Then Jesus straightened up, and said to her, "Woman, where are they has no one condemned you?" She replied, "No one, sir."

Then Jesus said, "Neither do I condemn you. Go, [and] from now on do not sin anymore.
John 8:1-11

One doubts Jesus approved of bloodshed or condoned murder or capital punishment. In this case, no one was free of sin and no one could pass judgment on her; neither did Jesus. It was also Jesus who said that not a single article of the law would pass from existence under him. To stone an adulterer and adulteress was still possible. Suppose the woman committed adultery again, would Jesus forgive her then? One thinks not. How many people have heard this history of how Jesus dealt with the woman and the crowd and how many have committed adultery despite the hearing? Probably a lot

The Marriage Bed

"Let marriage be honored among all and the marriage bed be kept undefiled, for God will judge the immoral and adulterers.
Hebrews 13:4

The man who dishonors his marriage bed says to himself, "Who can see me? Darkness surrounds me , walls hide me, no one sees me. Who can stop me from sinning?" He is not mindful of the Most High, fearing only humans eyes. He does not realize that the eyes of the Lord, ten thousand times brighter than the sun, Observe ever step taken and peer into hidden corners. The one who knows all things before they exists still knows them all after they are made. Such a man will be denounced in the streets of the city; and where he least suspects it, he will be apprehended. So it is with a woman unfaithful to her husband, who offers an heir by another man. First of all, she has disobeyed the law

of the Most High; second she has wronged her husband; Third, through her wanton adultery she has brought forth children by another man. Such a woman will be dragged before the assembly, and her punishment will extend to her children. Her children will not take root; her branches will not bring forth fruit. She will leave behind an accursed memory; her disgrace will never be blotted out.
Sirach 23:18-24

To Look at Another's Wife

"You have heard that it was said, 'You shall not commit adultery.' But I say to you, everyone who looks at a woman with lust has already committed adultery with her in his heart. If your right eye causes you to sin, tear it out and throw it away. It is better for you to lose one of your members than have your whole body thrown into Gehenna. And if you right hand causes you to sin, cut it off and throw it away. It is better for you to lose one of your members that to have your whole body go into Gehenna."

When you look lustfully at a woman married to someone else you steal something, the woman's sexuality, that belongs only to her husband. When you look at another's wife and imagine yourself sexually involved with her, while you have not committed physical adultery with her, you might have taken the first step towards it.

Jesus uses the loss of eye and loss of hand, not necessarily to mean to cut your hand or tear out your eye, to emphasize the gravity of lustful looks at someone who is not your mate. They are not to be taken lightly. Lustful looks lead to lustful thoughts, which lead to lustful actions. Adultery in many cases starts with a look.

Jesus also quite clearly states in these bible versus that adultery can lead to hell or Gehenna. Our sexual behavior when it involves people other than our spouses can be very destructive in this world and also lead to everlasting punishment in the next world.

We must therefore be very careful how we look at other peoples wive's, or if you are a woman, at other peoples husband's. Thoughts too must be disciplined to avoid adultery and lead to a fall. All adultery starts with a look, then a thought, then an action.

The society we live in is not Victorian and both women and men wear sexually provocative clothing. In fact the whole clothing industry oriented to make people physically and sexually attractive so that the above call to modesty and discipline is difficult if not nearly impossible.

Indeed television and movies, books, and magazines are oriented to be sexually provocative today. Models and actresses are often married. What is a person to do? One wonders if there are prayers strong enough to keep one from adulterous behavior. Maybe people should start with the one that has the line 'lead us not into temptation, but deliver us from evil'.

The bible has people who were involved in adulterous and near adulterous relationships and emphasizes their destructiveness. King David on his roof looked down on the naked Bathsheba who took a bath and lusted after her beauty. She came pregnant so David ordered the death or her husband, and took her as his wife. As a result David's line of family was forever cursed, he was guilty of murder, and the unborn child died. Again with the story of Joseph, Potiphar's wife lusted after Joseph, who had him put into prison when she lied about his behavior. With Susanna, the two lustful judges were put to death when their lusted after her. Lustful looks can lead to death in this world and hell in the next.

The Adultress

"By her eyelids and her haughty stare an unchaste wife can be recognized. Keep a strict watch over an unruly wife, lest, finding an opportunity, she make use of it; Follow close if her eyes are bold, and be not surprised if she betrays you; As a thirsty with eager mouth drinks from any water that he finds, So she settles down before any tent-peg, and opens her quiver for any arrow."

Sirach 26:9-12

A married man can have an adulterous relationship with a woman other than his wife, be she married, divorced or single. A married woman can have a relationship with a man who is not her husband be he married, single or divorced. There is also a possibility that the married man and married women are both having sexual and social relationships outside the marriage. The above biblical quote deals with the case of a woman who commits adultery with someone other than her husband.

This passage speaks of the care one must take to choose a wife. If one chooses a loose woman before marriage she will probably be a loose woman after marriage. The only precaution one can take when one marries a loose woman after marriage is to keep a strict watch over her, and even then there is the possibility that she will betray the marriage bed. She might have serial relationships outside of the marriage whenever the opportunity presents itself.

<u>Adultery One</u>

"Saving you from the wife of another, from the adulteress with her smooth words, Who forsakes the companion of her youth, and forgets the pact with her God; For her path sinks down to death, and her footsteps lead to the shades; None who enter thereon come back again, or walk the paths of life."

Proverbs 2:16-19

Marriage is an institution as old as man himself. It is the heart of the family and the foundation of all civilization. It is intended for the propagation of the species of man and to raise and train children. The basis of the family is the mutual love of husband and wife both emotionally and physically.

On television and newspapers today one reads of people who are married- that they have relationships with people other than their mates that is often sexual which tears at the fabric of a marriage. Perhaps this contributes to the over fifty percent divorce rate that is observed in today's society. The book of proverbs quoted above speaks specifically of when a woman strays from her marriage vows.

The adultery of today is often referred to as an affair, a word which softens the reality of this deadly sin. The woman, especially if attractive, breaks the relationship with her husband as she has a sexual relationship with another man- she forsakes the companion of her youth.

An adulterous relationship, strikes at the heart of a family to eliminate the trust one partner has in another. It frequently results in divorce. It often too results in death as an angry husband kills the man who commits the adultery or has him killed by someone else. Her footsteps do lead to the shades or hell, and none who enter thereon come back again, frequently killed by the jealous husband and certainly headed to hell.

The breech of trust is often permanent and cannot be repaired. Adultery is misplaced sexuality. It is when one is not satisfied with the sexual and emotional relationship with one partner. A person's "needs" are not met and they look to fulfill their lives elsewhere with someone else. Adultery can devastate a man and have serious repercussions on his life.

A love triangle as it is sometimes called effects three people, The adulteress, the adulterer, and the husband himself. In ancient times the woman was stoned to death because of her adulterous behavior. Today people are more entangled with divorce lawyers and psychologists and psychiatrists as their lives are realigned by the adulterous relationship. The husband too is filled with rage at another man who has tampered with his wife. For momentary pleasure, the adulterous male has risked his very life and his eternal soul. The deadly triangle the basis of which is two misplaced sensualities has also destroyed a marriage.

Warning Against Adultery

"My son, to my wisdom be attentive, to my knowledge incline your ear, That discretion may watch over you, and understanding may guard you. The lips of an adulteress drip with honey, and her mouth is smoother that oil; But in the end she is as bitter as wormwood, as sharp as a two-edged sword. Her feet do down to death, and to the nether world her steps attain; Lest you see before you the road to life, her paths will ramble, you know not where.

So now O children, listen to be, go not astray from the words of my mouth. Keep your way far from her, approach not the door of her house, Lest you give your honor to others, and you years to a merciless one; Lest strangers have their fill of your wealth, and your hard –won earnings go to an alien's house; And you groan in the end, when your flesh and your body are consumed; and you say, "Oh, why did I hate instruction, and my heart spurn reproof? Why did I not listen to the voice of my teachers, nor to my instructors incline my ear! I have all but come to utter ruin, condemned by the public assembly!"

"Drink Water from your own cistern, running water from your own well. How may your water sources be dispersed abroad, streams of water in the streets? Let you fountain be yours alone, and not one shared by strangers; And have joy of the wife of your youth, your lovely hind, your graceful doe. Her love will invigorate you always, through her love you will flourish continually, When you lie down she will watch over you, and when you wake, she will share your concerns; wherever you turn, she will guide you. Why then, my son, should you go astray for another's wife, and accept the embraces of an adulteress? For each man's ways are plain to the Lord's sight; all their path's he surveys; By his own iniquities the wicked man will be caught, in the meshes of his own sin he will be held fast; He will die from lack of discipline, through the greatness of his folly he will be lost"

Proverbs 5:1-23

<u>Warning Against Adultery II</u>

Observe, my son, your father's bidding, and reject not your mother's teaching; Keep them fastened over your heart always, put them around your neck; For the bidding is a lamp, and the teaching a light, and a way to life are the reproofs of discipline; To keep you from your neighbor's wife, from the smooth tongue of the adulteress. Lust not in your heart after her beauty, let her not captivate you with her glance! For the price of a loose woman may be scarcely a loaf of bread, But if she is married, she is a trap for your precious life. Can a man take fire into his bosom, and his garments not be scorched? So with him who goes to his neighbor's wife- none who touches her shall go unpunished. Men despise not the thief if he steals to satisfy his appetite when he is hungry; Yet if he is caught he must pay back sevenfold; all the wealth of his house he may yield up. But he who commits adultery is a fool; he who would destroy himself does it. A degrading beating he will get, and his disgrace will not be wiped away; For vindictive is the husband's wrath, he will have no pity on the day of vengeance; He will not consider any restitution, nor be satisfied with the greatest of gifts.

Proverbs 6:20-35

Warning Against Adultery III

My son, keep my words, and treasure my commands. Keep my commands and live, my teaching as the apple of your eye; Bind them on your fingers, write them on the tablet of your heart. Say to Wisdom, " You are my sister!" call Understanding, "Friend!" That they may keep you from another's wife, from the adulteress with her smooth words. For at the window of my house, through my lattice I looked out—And I saw among the simple ones, I observed among the young men, a youth with no sense, Going along the street near the corner, then walking in the

direction of her house—In the twilight, at dusk of day, at the time of the dark of night. And lo! The woman comes to meet him, robed like a harlot, with secret designs—She is fickle and unruly, in her home her feet cannot rest; Now she is in the streets, now in the open squares, and at every corner she lurks in ambush—When she seizes him, she kisses him, and with an impudent look says to him: "I owed peace offerings, and today I have fulfilled my vows; So I came out to meet you, to look for you, and I have found you! With coverlets I have spread my couch, and brocaded cloths of Egyptian linen; I have sprinkled my bed with myrrh, with aloes, and with cinnamon. Come let us drink our fill of love! For my husband is not at home, he has gone on a long journey; a bag of money he took with him, not till the full moon shall he return home." She wins him over by her repeated urging, with her smooth lips she leads him astray; He follows her stupidly, like an ox that is led to slaughter; Like a stag that minces toward the net, till an arrow pierces its liver; Like a bird that rushes into a snare, unaware that its life is at stake. So Now, O children, listen to me, be attentive to the words of my mouth! Let not your heart turn to her ways, go not astray in her paths; For many are those she has struck down dead, numerous, those she has slain. Her house is made up of ways in the nether world, leading down into the chambers of death.

Proverbs 7:1-27

To Look at Another's Wife

"You have heard that it was said, 'You shall not commit adultery.' But I say to you, everyone who looks at a woman with lust has already committed adultery with her in his heart. If your right eye causes you to sin, tear it out and throw it away. It is better for you to lose one of your members than have your whole body thrown into Gehenna. And if you right hand causes you to sin, cut it off and throw it away. It is better for you to lose one of your members that to have your whole body go into Gehenna."

When you look lustfully at a woman married to someone else you steal something, the woman's sexuality, that belongs only to her husband. When you look at another's wife and imagine yourself sexually involved with her, while you have not committed physical adultery with her, you might have taken the first step towards it.

Jesus uses the loss of eye and loss of hand, not necessarily to mean to cut your hand or tear out your eye, to emphasize the gravity of lustful looks at someone who is not your mate. They are not to be taken lightly. Lustful looks lead to lustful thoughts, which lead to lustful actions. Adultery in many cases starts with a look.

Jesus also quite clearly states in these bible versus that adultery can lead to hell or Gehenna. Our sexual behavior when it involves people other than our spouses can be very destructive in this world and also lead to everlasting punishment in the next world.

We must therefore be very careful how we look at other peoples wive's, or if you are a woman, at other peoples husband's. Thoughts too must be disciplined to avoid adultery and lead to a fall. All adultery starts with a look, then a thought, then an action.

The society we live in is not Victorian and both women and men wear sexually provocative clothing. In fact the whole clothing industry oriented to make people physically and sexually attractive so that the above call to modesty and discipline is difficult if not nearly impossible.

Indeed television and movies, books, and magazines are oriented to be sexually provocative today. Models and actresses are often married. What is a person to do? One wonders if there are prayers strong enough to keep one from adulterous behavior. Maybe people should start with the one that has the line 'lead us not into temptation, but deliver us from evil'.

The bible has people who were involved in adulterous and near adulterous relationships and emphasizes their destructiveness. King David on his roof looked down on the naked Bathsheba who took a bath and lusted after her beauty. She came pregnant so David ordered the death or her husband, and took her as his wife. As a result David's line of family was forever cursed, he was guilty of murder, and the unborn child died. Again with the story of Joseph, Potiphar's wife lusted after Joseph, who had him put into prison when she lied about his behavior. With Susanna, the two lustful judges were put to death when their lusted after her. Lustful looks can lead to death in this world and hell in the next.

Consequences to Sexuality Outside of Marriage

There are many consequences to sexuality outside of the life-affirming contract of matrimony. These include sterility, abortion, and sexually transmitted disease.

Many people who have sexual relations outside of marriage conceive children they cannot afford or do not want. Tragically many of the pregnancies result in abortion—the destruction of innocent human life.

Another complication of sex outside of marriage is unwanted sterility—the inability of people to bear children when people want them. This may occur in both men and women and is usually the result of sexually transmitted diseases like gonorrhea.

Sexually transmitted diseases are also a consequence of sex outside of marriage, whether it be a teenager who has sex with another teenager, and man or woman who has sexual relations outside their marriage, and a divorced person who has sex with another, every one who has sexual relations with a person different from their spouse is susceptible to these plagues. Sexually transmitted diseases include syphilis, gonorrhea, chlamydia, herpes, Human Immune Virus, and a host of others.

The Commandment
"You shall not commit adultery"
Exodus 20:14

"You shall not have carnal relations with your neighbors wife, defiling yourself with her"
Leviticus 18:20

"If a man is discovered having relations with a woman who is married to another, both the man and the woman with whom she has had relations shall die. Thus shall you purge the evil from your midst."

Deuteronomy 22:22

The above laws made it quite clear that when a married man or woman had relations with someone other than their spouse that they committed adultery. It also made clear that when anyone whether they were married, divorced, or single and never married had sexual relations with some one who was married then that person was guilty of adultery. Adultery was prohibited by the ten commandments. Adultery was punishable by death in the ancient world. Both the married person and the other person whether divorces, married, or single were to be put to death. There was no double penalty for a married man or woman having relations with another persons wife or husband although there probably should be.

The law was meant to protect the institution of marriage, to insure offspring were of one couple only, and to prevent the transmission of sexually transmitted diseases. The law was also meant to make sure that the family was holy in the presence of God.

The command against adultery was so important that it was included with the ten primary ones so that it was absolutely followed by the people. To some extent the command was repeated in the last commandment that you shall not covet thy neighbors wife.

DIVORCE

This also you do: the altar of the Lord you cover with tears weeping and groaning. Because he no longer regards you sacrifice nor accepts it favorably from your hand; And you say, "Why is it?"—Because the Lord is witness between you and the wife of your youth, With whom you have broken faith though she is your companion, your betrothed wife. Did he not make one being, with flesh and spirit: and what does that one require but godly offspring? You must then safeguard life that is your own, and not break faith with the wife of your youth. For I hate divorce , says the LORD, the God of Israel, And covering one's garment with injustice, says the LORD of hosts; You must then safeguard life that is your own, and not break faith.
Malachi 213-16

To the married, however, I give this instruction (not I , but the Lord): A wife should not separate from her husband—and if she does separate she must either remain single or become reconciled to her husband—and a husband should not divorce his wife.
1 Corinthians 7: 10-11

"For this reason a man shall leave [his] father and mother and be joined to his wife, and the two shall become one flesh."

Ephesians 5:31

To the married, however, I give this instruction (not I, but the Lord): a wife should not separate from her husband—and if she does separate she must either remain single or become reconciled to her husband—and a husband should not divorce his wife.

1 Corinthians 7: 10-11

When Jesus finished these words, he left Galilee and went to the district of Judea across the Jordan. Great crowds followed him, and he cured them there. Some Pharisees approached him, and tested him, saying, "Is it lawful for a man to divorce his wife for any cause whatever?" He said in reply, "Have you not read that from the beginning , the Creator 'made them male and female' and said, 'For this reason a man shall leave his father and mother and be joined to his wife, and the two shall become one flesh'? So they are no longer two but one flesh. Therefore, what God has joined together, no human must separate." They said to him, "then why did Moses command that the man give the woman a bill of divorce and dismiss [her]?" He said to them , "Because of the hardness of your hearts Moses allowed you to divorce your wives, but from the beginning it was not so. I say to you, whoever divorces his wife (unless the marriage is unlawful) and marries another commits adultery." [His] disciples said to him, "If that is the case of a man with his wife, is it better not to marry." He answered, "Not all can accept [this] word, but only those to whom that is granted. Some are incapable of marriage because they were born so; some, because they were made so by others; some, because

they have renounced marriage for the sake of the kingdom of heaven. Whoever can accept this ought to accept it."
Matthew 19:1-12

According to this new testament letter if two people married to each other suffer difficulties they are unable to surmount and wish to divorce then they should not divorce but separate. There is no cause that justifies divorce if two people have married according to the teachings of Jesus except for discovered incest- that two people discover they are closely related. Jesus overturned the teaching and law of Moses that a man could offer a bill of divorce to a woman. Divorce was no longer acceptable under the teaching of Jesus.

Married people should separate when they have insurmountable difficulties. One supposes that this means that they live in separate households. If and when these difficulties are resolved, they can subsequently reunite. The problems that can arise in marriage are many. Sometimes problems are so overwhelming that the married couple are unable to withstand them.

In the Catholic Church, a six month to one year waiting period is required before two people can marry. This allows a necessary period of courtship where people can evaluate whether they are suitable for one another. The courtship period allows for each person to see whether the couple can accommodate the problems and defects in the other person- To see whether in fact they are compatible. A person should enter marriage with little if any emotional baggage and try and solve as many major and minor problems they have before entering marriage.

Two people should take seriously the marriage vows they have made to one another when they begin marriage and throughout the course of their marriage- for better or for worse, in richness and in poverty, in sickness and in health. Marriage is not always a picnic.

A cooling off period and ceasefire in the form of separation can allow the family and married couple to heal so that they can come back to the marriage. Sometimes the marriage is stronger after the separation. By not means should they divorce, and in accord with the teachings of Jesus neither should ever remarry unless their spouse dies.

Psychological counseling or psychiatric treatment may aid the separated couple define issues, solve problems, and overcome difficulties. Marriage encounter groups, get away weekends and the like sometimes help families. Children should be allowed to see both parents in a separation. Some times multiple separations separated by time may be required in a marriage. If the obstacles to a successful and fruitful marriage are too much to overcome to couple should remain separated. Neither should divorce and none should remarry. Both separately should try to help raise the children of the marriage.

Marriage lasts as long as the people who took vows live. While their will be no marriage in heaven, and sexual roles and marriage roles will be transcended. There, people at least can try for happiness here. There will probably be a lot of people who divorced and remarried in hell.

Divorce and Adultery

"It was also said, 'Whoever divorces his wife must give her a bill of divorce.' But I say to you, whoever divorces his wife (unless the marriage is unlawful) causes her to commit adultery, and who ever marries a divorces woman commits adultery."

Matthew 5:31-32

"Everyone who divorces his wife and marries another commits adultery, and the one who marries a woman divorced from her husband commits adultery."

Luke 16:18

When Jesus finished these words, he left Galilee and went to the district of Judea across the Jordan. Great crowds followed him, and he cured them there. Some Pharisees approached him, and tested him, saying, "Is it lawful for a man to divorce his wife for any cause whatsoever?" He said in reply, "Have you not read that from the beginning the Creator 'made them male and female' and said for this reason a man shall leave his father and mother and be joined to his wife, and the two shall become one flesh'? Therefore, what God has joined together, no human being must separate." They said to him, "Then why did Moses command that the man give the woman a bill of divorce and dismiss her?" He said to them, " Because of the hardness of your hearts Moses allowed you to divorce your wives, but from the beginning it was not so. I say to you, who ever divorces his wife (unless the marriage is unlawful) and marries another commits adultery."

Matthew 19:1-9

He set out from there and went into the district of Judea across the Jordan. Again crowds gathered around him and, as was his custom, he again taught them. The Pharisees approached and asked "Is it lawful for a husband to divorce his wife?" They were testing him. He said to them in reply, "What did Moses command you?" They replied, "Moses permitted him to write a bill of divorce and dismiss her." But Jesus told them, "Because of the hardness of your hearts he wrote you this commandment. But from the beginning of creation, 'God made them male and female. For this reason a man shall leave his father and mother [and be joined to his wife], and the two shall become one flesh. So they are no longer two but one flesh. Therefore what God has joined together, no human being must separate." In the house the disciples again questioned him about this. He said to them, "Whoever divorces his wife and marries another commits adultery against her; and if she divorces her husband and marries another she commits adultery."

Mark 10:1-12

So important was the teaching of Jesus on the subject of divorce that it was included in three of the Gospels. Jesus states explicitly that a man who divorces his wife and marries another woman commits adultery; that a woman who divorces her husband and marries another man commits adultery; and that a man who marries a woman divorced from her husband commits adultery. Presumably a woman who marries a man divorced from his wife also commits adultery.

Jesus made it clear that divorce was prohibited with the sole exclusion being porneie or incest among the two who were married- that people who married one another should not divorce. Jesus also stated that Moses decree that allowed divorce was not as God intended for husband and wife were one flesh that should not be separated by anyone. The only way out of a marriage was to be the natural death of a partner in which case the widow or widower could remarry.

Divorce

When Jesus finished these words, he left Galilee and went to the district of Judea across the Jordan. Great crowds followed him, and he cured them there. Some Pharisees approached him, and tested him, saying, "Is it lawful for a man to divorce his wife for any cause whatever?" He said in reply, " Have you not read that from the beginning the Creator 'made them male and female' and said, 'For this reason a man shall leave his father and mother and be joined to his wife, and the two shall become one flesh'? So they are no longer two but one flesh. Therefore, what God has joined together, no human being must separate." They said to him, " Then why did Moses command that the man give the woman a bill of divorce and dismiss [her]?" He said to them, "Because of the hardness of your hearts, Moses allowed you to divorce your wives, but from the beginning it was not so. I say to you, whoever divorces his wife (unless the marriage was unlawful) and marries another commits adultery." [His} disciples said to him, "If this is the case of a man with his wife, it is better not to marry." He answered, " Not all can accept [this] word but only those to whom that is granted. Some are incapable of marriage because they were born so; some because they were made so by others; some, because they have renounced marriage for the sake of the kingdom of heaven. Whoever can accept this ought to accept it."

Matthew 19:1-12

The Pharisees approached and asked, "Is it lawful for a husband to divorce his wife?" They were testing him. He said to them in reply, "What did Moses command you?" They replied, " Moses permitted him to write a bill of divorce and dismiss her." But Jesus told them, "Because of the harness of your hearts he wrote you this commandment. But from the beginning of creation, 'God made them male and female. For this reason a man shall leave his father and mother [and be joined to his wife], and the two shall become one flesh. Therefore what God has joined together, no human being must separate." In the house the disciples again questioned him about this. He said to them, "Whoever divorces his wife and marries another commits adultery against her; and if she divorces her husband and marries another, she commits adultery."

Mark 10:2-12

"It was also said, "whoever divorces his wife must give her a bill of divorce. But I say to you, whoever divorces his wife (unless the marriage is unlawful) causes her to commit adultery, and whoever marries a divorces woman commits adultery."

Matthew 5:31-32

To the married, however, I give this instruction (not I, but the Lord): a wife should not separate from her husband—and if she does separate she must either remain single or become reconciled to her husband—and a husband should not divorce his wife.

1 Corinthians 7: 10-11

According to this new testament letter if two people married to each other suffer difficulties they are unable to surmount and wish to divorce then they should not divorce but separate. There is no cause that justifies divorce if two people have married according to the teachings of Jesus except for discovered incest- that two people discover they are closely related. Jesus overturned the teaching and law of Moses that a man could offer a bill of divorce to a woman.

Divorce was no longer acceptable under the teaching of Jesus.

Married people should separate when they have insurmountable difficulties. One supposes that this means that they live in separate households. If and when these difficulties are resolved, they can subsequently reunite. The problems that can arise in marriage are many. Sometimes problems are so overwhelming that the married couple are unable to withstand them.

In the Catholic Church, a six month to one year waiting period is required before two people can marry. This allows a necessary period of courtship where people can evaluate whether they are suitable for one another. The courtship period allows for each person to see whether the couple can accommodate the problems and defects in the other person- To see whether in fact they are compatible. A person should enter marriage with little if any emotional baggage and try and solve as many major and minor problems they have before entering marriage.

Two people should take seriously the marriage vows they have made to one another when they begin marriage and throughout the course of their marriage- for better or for worse, in richness and in poverty, in sickness and in health. Marriage is not always a picnic.

A cooling off period and ceasefire in the form of separation can allow the family and married couple to heal so that they can come back to the marriage. Sometimes the marriage is stronger after the separation. By not means should they divorce, and in accord with the teachings of Jesus neither should ever remarry unless their spouse dies.

Psychological counseling or psychiatric treatment may aid the separated couple define issues, solve problems, and overcome difficulties. Marriage encounter groups, get away weekends and the like sometimes help families. Children should be allowed to see both parents in a separation. Some times multiple separations separated by time may be required in a marriage. If the obstacles to a successful and fruitful marriage are too much to overcome to couple should remain separated. Neither should divorce and none should remarry. Both separately should try to help raise the children of the marriage.

Marriage lasts as long as the people who took vows live. While their will be no marriage in heaven, and sexual roles and marriage roles will be transcended. There, people at least can try for happiness here. There will probably be a lot of people who divorced and remarried in hell.

WIDOWS

Are you unaware, brothers (for I am speaking to people who know the law), that the law had jurisdiction over one as long as one lives? Thus a married woman is bound by law to her living husband; but if her husband dies, she is released from the law in respect to her husband. Consequently, while her husband is alive she will be called an adulteress if she consorts with another man. But if her husband dies she is free from that law, and she is not an adulteress is she consorts with another man.
Romans 7:1-3

A wife is bound to her husband as long a he lives. But if her husband dies, she is free to be married to whomever she wishes, provided that it be in the Lord. She is more blessed, though in my opinion, if she remains as she is, and I think that I too have the Spirit of God.
1 Corinthians 7:39-40

Honor widows who are truly widows. But if a widow has children or grandchildren, let these first learn to perform their religious duty to their own family and to make recompense to their parents for this is pleasing to God. The real widow who is all alone, has set her hope on

God and continues in supplications and prayers night and day. But the one who is self-indulgent is dead while she lives. Command this, so that they may be irreproachable. And whoever does not provide for relatives and especially family members has denied the faith and is worse than an unbeliever.

Let a widow be enrolled if she is not less than sixty years old, married only once, with a reputation for good works, namely that she has raised children, practiced hospitality, washed the feet of the holy ones, helped those in distress, involved herself in every good work. But exclude younger widows, for when their sensuality estranges them from Christ, they want to marry and will incur condemnation for breaking their first pledge. And furthermore, they learn to be idlers, going about from house to house, and not only idlers but gossips and busybodies as well, talking about things that ought not to be mentioned. So I would like younger widows to marry, have children and manage a home, so as to give the adversary no pretext for maligning us. For some have already turned away to follow Satan. If any woman believer has widowed relatives, she must assist them; the church is not to be burdened, so that it will be able to help those who are truly widows.

1 Timothy 5:3-16

Ruth

Once in the time of the judges there was a famine in the land; so a man from Bethlehem of Judah departed with his wife and two sons to reside on the plateau of Moab. The man was named Elimelech, his wife Naomi, and his sons Mahlon and Chilion; they were Ephrathites from Bethlehem of Judah. Some time after their arrival on the

⚜ GOD & SEX ⚜

Moabite plateau, Elimelech, the husband of Naomi died, and she was left with her two sons, who married Moabite women, one named Orpah, the other Ruth. When they had lived their about ten years, both Mahlon and Chilion died also, and the woman was left with neither her two sons nor her husband. She then made ready to go back from the plateau of Moab because word reached her there that the LORD had visited his people and given them food.

She and her two daughters-in-law left the place where they had been living. Then as they were on the road back to the land of Judah, Naomi dais to her two daughters-in-law, "Go back, each of you, to your mother's house! May the LORD be kind to you as you were to the departed and to me! May the LORD grant each of you a husband and a home in which you will find rest." She kissed them good-by, but they wept with loud sobs, and told her they would return with her to her people. "Go back, my daughters!" said Naomi. "Why should you come with me? Have I other sons in my womb who may become your husbands? Go back, my daughters! Go for I am too old to marry again. And even if I could offer any hopes, or if tonight I had a husband if I could offer any hopes, or if tonight I had a husband or had borne sons, would you then wait and deprive yourselves of husbands until those sons grew up? No my daughters! My lot is too bitter for you, because the LORD has extended his hand against me." Again they sobbed and wept; and Orpah kissed her mother-in-law good-by, but Ruth stayed with her.

"See now!" she said, "your sister-in-law has gone back to her people and her god. Go back after your sister-in law!" But Ruth said, "Do not ask me to abandon or forsake you! for wherever you go I will go, wherever you lodge, I will lodge, your people shall be my people, and your God my God. Wherever you die I will die, and there be buried. May the Lord do so and so to me, and more besides, if aught but death separates me from you!" Naomi then ceased to urge her, for she saw she was determined to go with her.

So they went on together till they reached Bethlehem. On their arrival their, the whole city was astir over them, and the women asked, " Can this be Naomi?. But she said to them, " Do not call me Naomi. Call me Mara, for the almighty has made it very bitter for me. I went away with an abundance, but the Lord has brought me back destitute. Why should you call me Naomi, since the Lord has brought evil upon me?" Thus it was that Naomi returned with her Moabite, daughter in law Ruth, who accompanied her back from the plateau of Moab. They arrived in Bethlehem at the beginning of the Barley Harvest.

Naomi had a prominent kinsman named Boaz, of the clan or her husband Elimelech. Ruth the Moabite said to Naomi. "Let me go and glean ears of grain in the field of anyone who will allow me that favor." Naomi said to her, "Go, my daughter," and she went. The field she entered to glean after the Harvesters happened to be the section belonging to Boaz of the clan of Elimelech. Boaz himself came from Bethlehem and said to the Harvesters, "The Lord be with you!" and they replied, "The Lord bless you!" Boaz asked the overseer of the harvesters, "Whose girl is this?" The overseer of the harvesters answered, "She is the Moabite girl who returned from the plateau of Moab with Naomi. She asked leave to gather the gleanings into sheaves after the harvesters; and ever since she came this morning she has remained here until now, with scarcely a moment's rest."

Boaz said to Ruth, "Listen my daughter! Do not go to glean in anyone else's field; you are not to leave here. Stay here with my women servants. Watch to see which field is to be harvested, and follow them; I have commanded the young men to do you no harm. When you are thirsty, you may go and drink from the vessels the young men have filled." Casting herself prostate upon the ground she said to him, " Why should I, a foreigner, be favored with your notice?" Boaz answered her: "I have had a complete account of what you have done for your mother-in-law after your husband's death; you have left your father and your mother and the land of your birth, and have come to a people you did not know previously. May the Lord Reward what you have done! May you receive a full reward from the God of Israel, under whose wings you have come for refuge." She said, "May I prove worthy of your kindness, my lord: you have comforted me, your servant, with your consoling words: would indeed that I were a servant of yours!" At mealtime Boaz said to her," Come here and have some food; dip your bread in the sauce." Then as she sat near the reapers, he handed her some roasted grain and she ate her fill and had some left over. She rose to glean, and Boaz instructed his servants to let her glean among the sheaves themselves without scolding her, and even to let drop some handfuls and leave them for her to glean without being rebuked.

She gleaned in the field until evening, and when she beat out what she had gleaned it came to about an ephah of Barley, which she took into the city and showed to her mother-and-law. Next she brought out and gave her what she had left over from lunch. So her mother-in-law said to her, "Where did you glean today? Where did you go to work? May he who took notice of you be blessed!" Then she told her mother-in-law with whom she had worked. "The man at whose place I worked today is named Boaz," she said. "may he be blessed by the LORD, who is ever merciful to the living and the dead," Naomi exclaimed to her daughter in law; and she continued, "He is a relative of ours, one of our next of kin." "He even told me ," added Ruth the Moabite, "that I should stay with his servants until they complete his entire harvest." You would do well, my dear," Naomi rejoined, " to go out with his servant's; for in someone else's field you might be insulted." So she stayed gleaning with the servants of Boaz until the end of the Barley and wheat harvests.

When she was back with her mother-in-law, Naomi said to her, "My daughter, I must seek a home for you that will please you. Now is not Boaz, with whose servants you were, a relative of ours? This evening he will be winnowing barley at the threshing floor. So bathe and anoint yourself; then put on your best attire and go down to the threshing floor. Do not make yourself known to the man before he has finished eating and drinking. But when he lies down, take note of the place where he does so. Then go, uncover a place at his feet, and lie down. He will tell you what to do." "I will do whatever you advise," Ruth replied. So she went down to the threshing floor and did just as her mother-in-law had instructed her.

Boaz ate and drank to his heart's content. Then when he went and lay down at the edge of the sheaves, she stole up, uncovered a place at his feet, and lay down. IN the middle of the night, however the man gave a start and turned around to find a woman lying at his feet. He asked, "Who are you?" And she replied, "I am your servant Ruth. Spread the corned of your cloak over me, for you are my next of kin." He said, "May the LORD bless you, my daughter! You have been even more loyal now than before in not going after the young men, whether poor or rich. So be assured, daughter, I will do for you whatever you say; all my townspeople know you are a worthy woman. Now, though indeed I am closely related to you, you have another relative still closer. Stay as you are for tonight, and tomorrow, if he wished to claim you, good! Let him do so. But if he does not wish to claim you, as the LORD lives, I will claim you myself. Lie there until morning." So she lay at his feet until morning , but rose before men could recognize one another. Boaz said, " Let it not be known that this woman came to the threshing floor." Then he said to her, " Take off your cloak and hold it out." When she did so, he poured out six measures of barley, helped her lift the bundle, and left for the city.

Ruth went home to her mother-in-law, who asked, "How have you fared, my daughter?" So she told her all the man had done for her, and concluded, " He gave me these six measures of barley because he did not wish me to come back to my mother-in-law empty handed!" Naomi then said, "Wait here my daughter, until you learn what happens, for the man will not rest, but will settle the matter today."

Boaz went and took a seat at the gate; and when he saw the closer relative of whom he had spoken come along, he called to him by name, "Come and sit beside me!" And he did so. Then Boaz picked out ten of the elders of the city and asked them to sit nearby. When they had done this, he said to the near relative: "Naomi, who has come back from the Moabite plateau, is putting up for sale the piece of land that belonged to our kinsman Elimelech. So I thought I would inform you, bidding you before those here present, including the elders of my people, to put in your claim for it if you wish to acquire it as next of kin. But if you do not wish to claim it, tell me so, that I may be guided accordingly, for no one has a prior claim to yours, and mine is next." He answered, "I will put in my claim."

Boaz continued, "Once you acquire the field from Naomi, you must take also Ruth the Moabite, the widow of the late heir, and raise up a family for the departed on his estate. "The near relative replied, "I cannot exercise by claim lest I depreciate my own estate. Put in a claim yourself in my stead, for I cannot exercise my claim. Now it used to be the custom in Israel that, to make binding a contract of redemption or exchange, one party would take off his sandal and give it to the other. This was the form of attestation in Israel. So the near relative, in saying to Boaz, "Acquire it for yourself," drew off his sandal. Boaz then said to the elders and to all the people, " You are witnesses today that I have acquired from Naomi all the holdings of Elimelech, Chilion, and Mahlon. I also take Ruth the Moabite, the widow of Mahlon, as my wife, in order to raise up a family for her late husband on his estate, so that the name of the departed may not perish among his kinsmen and fellow citizens. Do you witness this today?" All those at the gate, including the elders, said, "We do so. May the Lord make this wife come into your house like Rachel and Leah, who between them built up the house of Israel. May you do well in Ephrathah and win fame in Bethlehem. With the offspring the Lord will give you from this girl, may your house become like the house of Perez, who Tamar bore to Judah."

Boaz took Ruth. When they came together as man and wife, the LORD enabled her to conceive and she bore a son. Then the women said to Naomi, "Blessed is the LORD who has not failed to provide you today with an heir! May he become famous in Israel! He will be your comfort and the support of your old age, for his mother is the daughter-in-law who loves you. She is worth more to you than seven sons!" Naomi took the child, placed him on her lap, and became his nurse. And the neighbor women gave him his name, at the news that a grandson had been born to Naomi. They called him Obed. He was father of Jesse, the father of David.

These are the descendants of Perez: Perez was the father of Hezron, Hezron was the father of Ram, Ram was the father of Amminadab, Amminadab was the father of Nahshon, Nahshon was the father of Salmon, Salmon was the father of Boaz, Boaz was the father of Obed, Obed was the father of Jesse, and Jesse became the father of David.

VIRGINITY

When a man seduces a virgin who is not betrothed and lies with her, he shall pay her marriage price and marry her, If her father refuses to give her to him, he still must pay the customary marriage price for virgins.

Exodus 22:15-16

If a man comes upon a maiden that is not betrothed, takes her and has relations with her, and their deed is discovered, the man who had relations with her shall pay the girl's father fifty silver shekels and take her as his wife because he has deflowered her. Moreover, he may not divorce her as long as he lives.

Deuteronomy 22:28-29

Then the kingdom of heaven will be like ten virgins who took their lamps and went out to meet the bridegroom. Five of them were foolish and five were wise. The foolish ones, when taking their lamps, brought no oil with them, but the wise brought flasks of oil with their lamps. Since the bridegroom was long delayed, they all became drowsy and fell asleep. At midnight, there was a cry, 'Behold the bridegroom! Come out to meet him!' Then all those virgins got up and trimmed their lamps. The foolish ones said to the wise, 'Give us some of your oil, for our lamps are going out.' But the wise ones replied, 'NO, for there may not be enough for us and for you. Go instead to the merchants and buy some for yourselves.' While they went off to buy it, the bridegroom came and those who ere ready went into the wedding feats with him. Then the door was locked. Afterwards the other virgins came and said, 'Lord, Lord open the door for us!' But he said in reply, 'Amen, I say to you, I do not know you.' Therefore, stay awake, for you know neither the day nor the hour.

Matthew 25:1-13

Now in regard to virgins, I have no commandment from the Lord, but I give my opinion as one who by the Lord's mercy is trustworthy. So this is what I think best because of the present distress: that it is a good thing for a person to remain as he is. Are you bound to a wife? Do not seek a separation. Are you free of a wife? Then do not look for a wife. If you marry, however, you do not sin , nor does an un married woman sin if she marries; but such people will experience affliction in their earthly life, and I would like to spare you that.

I tell you, brothers, the time is running out. From now on, let those having wives act as not having them, those weeping as not weeping, those rejoicing and not rejoicing, those buying as not owning, those using the world as not using it fully. For the world in its present form is passing away.

I should like you to be free of anxieties. An unmarried man is anxious about the things of the Lord, how he may please the Lord. But a married man is anxious about the things of the world, how he may please his wife, and he is divided. An unmarried woman or a virgin is anxious about the things of the Lord, so that she might be holy in both body and spirit. A married woman, on the other hand, is anxious about the things of the world, how she may please her husband. I am telling you this for your own benefit, not to impose a restraint upon you, but for the sake of propriety and adherence to the Lord without distraction.

If anyone thinks he is behaving improperly towards his virgin, and a critical moment has come and so it has to be, let him do as he wishes. He is committing no sin; let them get married. The one who stands firm in his resolve however, who is not under compulsion but has power over his own will, and has made up his mind to keep his virgin, will be doing well. So then, the one who marries his virgin does well; the one who does not marry her will do better.

1 Corinthians 7:25-38

Then I looked and there was the Lamb standing on Mount Zion, and with him a hundred and forty-four thousand who had his name and his Father's name written on their foreheads. I heard a sound from heaven like the sound of rushing water or a loud peal of thunder. The sound I heard was like that of harpists playing their harps. They were singing [what seemed to be] a new hymn before the throne, before the four living creatures and the elders. No one could learn this hymn except the hundred and forty-four thousand who had been ransomed from the earth. These are they who were not defiled with women; they are virgins and these are the ones who follow the lamb wherever he goes. They have been ransomed as the first fruits of the human race for God and the Lamb. On Their lips no deceit has been found; they are unblemished.

Revelation 14:1-5

HOMOSEXUALITY

<u>Sodom and Gomorrah</u>

The two angels reached Sodom in the evening, as Lot was sitting at the gate of Sodom. When Lot saw them, he got up to greet them; and bowing down with his face to the ground, he said, "Please gentlemen, come inside into your servant's house for the night, and bathe your feet; you can get up early to continue your journey." But they replied, "No, we shall pass the night in the town square." He urged them so strongly, however, that they turned aside to his place and entered his house. He prepared a meal for them, baking cakes without leaven , and they dined.

Before they went to bed, all the townsmen of Sodom, both young and old—all the people to the last man—closed in on the house. They called to Lot and said to him, " Where are the men who came to your house tonight? Bring them out to us that we may have intimacies with them." Lot went out to meet them at the entrance. When he had shut the door behind him, he said, " I beg you, my brothers, not to do this wicked thing. I have two daughters who have never had intercourse with men. Let me bring them out to you, and you may do to them as

you please. But don't do anything to these men, for you know they have come under the shelter of my roof." They replied, " Stand back! This fellow," they sneered, " came here as an immigrant, and he now dares to give orders! We'll treat you worse than them!" With that, they pressed down the door. But his guests put out their hands, pulled Lot inside with them, and closed the door; at the same time they struck the men at the entrance of the house, one and all, with such a blinding light that they were utterly unable to reach the doorway.

Then the angels said to Lot: "Who else belongs to you here? Your sons (sons-in –law) and your daughters and all who belong to you in the city—take them away from it! We are about to destroy this place, for the outcry reaching the LORD against those in the city is so great that he has sent us to destroy it." So Lot went out and spoke to his sons- in-law who had contracted marriage with his daughters. "Get up and leave this place," he told them; "the LORD is about to destroy the city." But his sons-in-law thought he was joking.

As dawn was breaking, the angels urged Lot on, saying, "On your way! Take with you your wife and your two daughters who are here, or you will be swept away in the punishment of the city." When he hesitated, the men by the LORD's mercy, seized his hand and the hands of his wife and two daughters and led them to safety outside the city. As soon as they had been brought outside, he was told: "Flee for your life! Don't look back or stop anywhere on the Plain. Get off to the hills at once, or you will be swept away." "Oh, no, my lord!" "You have already thought enough of your servant to do me the great kindness of saving my life. But I cannot flee to the hills to keep the disaster from overtaking me, and so I shall die. Look, this town ahead is near enough to escape to. It's only a small place. Let me flee there—it's a small place isn't it? – that my life may be saved." "Well then," he replied, "I will also grant you the favor you now ask. I will not overthrow the town you speak of. Hurry, escape, there! I cannot do anything until you arrive there." That is why the town is called Zoar.

The sun was just rising over the earth as Lot arrived in Zoar; at the same time the LORD rained down sulphurous fire upon Sodom and Gomorrah (from the LORD out of heaven) He overthrew those cities and the whole plain, together with the inhabitants of the cities, and the produce of the soil. But Lot's wife looked back, and she was turned into a pillar of salt.

Early the next morning Abraham went to the place where he had stood in the LORD's presence. As he looked down toward Sodom and Gomorrah and the whole region of the Plain, he saw dense smoke over the land rising like fumes from a furnace.

Thus it came to pass: when God destroyed the Cities of the Plain, he was mindful of Abraham by sending Lot away from the upheaval by which God overthrew the cities where Lot had been living.

Genesis 19:1-29

The Punishment of Idolaters

The wrath of God is indeed being revealed from heaven against every impiety and wickedness of those who suppress the truth by their wickedness.. For what can be known about God is evident to them, because God made it evident to them. Ever since the creation of the world, his invisible attributes of eternal power and divinity have been able to be understood and perceived in what he has made. As a result, they have no excuse; for although they knew God they did not accord him glory as God or give him thanks. Instead, they became vain in their reasoning, and their senseless minds were darkened. While claiming to be wise, they became fools and exchanged the glory of the immortal God for the likeness of an image of mortal man or of birds or of four-legged animals or of snakes.

Therefore, God handed them over to impurity through the lust of their hearts for the mutual degradation of their bodies. They exchanged the truth of God for a lie and revered and worshiped the creature rather than the creator, who is blessed forever. Amen. Therefore God handed them over to degrading passions. Their females exchanged natural relations for unnatural, and the males likewise gave up natural relations with females and burned with lust for one another. Males did shameful things with males and thus received in their own persons the due penalty for their perversity. And since they did not see fit to acknowledge God, God handed then over to their undiscerning mind to do what is improper. They are filled with every form of wickedness, evil, greed, and malice; full of envy, murder, rivalry, treachery, and spite. They are gossips and scandalmongers and they hate God. They are insolent, haughty, boastful, ingenious in their wickedness, and rebellious towards their parents. They are senseless, faithless, heartless, ruthless. Although they know the just degree of God that all who practice such things deserve death, they not only do them but give approval to those who practice them.

Romans 1:18-32

You shall not lie with a male as with a woman; such thing is an abomination.

Leviticus 18:22

If a man lies with a male as with a woman, both of them shall be put to death for their abominable deed; they have forfeited their lives.

Leviticus 20:13

Do you not know that the unjust will not inherit the kingdom of God? Do not be deceived; neither fornicators nor idolaters nor adulterers nor boy prostitutes nor sodomites nor thieves nor the greedy nor drunkards nor slanderers nor robbers will inherit the kingdom of God.

1 Corinthians 6:9-10

Practicing male homosexuals-those who engage in anal intercourse or stick their penis's in other men's anus's and rectums are abhorrent to God. The book of Leviticus in the bible states that they should receive the death penalty. Bi-sexuals who have sex with men and women should also be killed.

Practicing male homosexuals reap the scourge of the flesh as they get HIV-AIDS, hepatitis, gonorrhea, syphilis, chlymidae, genital herpes, and many other venereal diseases. They can also get perforated rectums, hemorrhoids, and anal fissures.

Most importantly practicing male homosexuals go to hell for eternity if they do not stop and repent of their sins.

Biblical teaching on homosexuality and Catholic teaching which says that homosexuality is gravely disordered and perverse is in constant conflict with the teaching and acceptance of the world. In today's culture, homosexuality is considered acceptable and a variant of normal. Men are allowed to marry other men, and the sodomy laws are nullified. Governments and courts have given their stamp of approval to homosexual behavior and it has become a protected form of behavior.

Natural law however is never defeated and despite man's intent to erase God's law on this matter, his wrath has prevailed. Hundreds of thousands of male homosexuals have died of HIV-AIDS and millions more are infected with the virus and will die.

Sodomites who have abused young boys and children have been given jail terms and punished with multimillion dollar verdicts against them.

It is said that ten percent of the society in the United States are active practicing homosexuals. Perhaps United States will suffer the fate of Sodom and Gomorrah.

How we express of sexuality is important not only to ourselves, but also to each other and to God. Homosexuality that is practiced between men is abhorrent to God. He is so offended by it that he wants practicing homosexuals condemned to death. When whole communities practiced it like in Sodom and Gomorrah and the cities on the plain, he destroyed them all. Homosexuality is abhorrent to God because it uses excretory organs for sexual pleasure. It is also abhorrent to God because it is non-creative and does not result in the issuance of infants and children. It is unnatural and defies the natural law.

RAPE

The Rape of Dinah

Dinah, the daughter who Leah had borne to Jacob, went out to visit some of the women of the land. When Shechem, son of Hamor the Hivite, who was chief of the region, saw her, he seized her and lay with her by force. Since he was strongly attracted to Dinah, daughter of Jacob, indeed was really in love with the girl, he endeavored to win her affection. Shechem also asked his father Hamor, "Get me this girl as a wife."

Meanwhile, Jacob heard that Shechem had defiled his daughter Dinah; but since his sons were out in the fields with his livestock, he held his peace until they came home. Now Hamor, the father of Shechem, went out to discuss the matter with Jacob, just as Jacob's sons were coming in from the fields. When they heard the news, the men were shocked and seethed with indignation. What Shechem had done was an outrage in Israel; such a thing could not be tolerated.

Hamor appealed to them, saying, "My son Shechem, has his heart set on your daughter. Please give her to him in marriage. Intermarry with us; give your daughters to us, and take your daughters for yourselves. Thus you can live among us. The land is open before you; you can settle and move about freely in it, and acquire landed property here. Then Shechem, too, appealed to Dinah's father and brothers: "Do me this favor, and I will pay whatever you demand of me. No matter how high you set the bridal price. I will pay you whatever you ask; only give me the maiden in marriage."

Jacob's son's replied to Shechem and his father Hamor with guile, speaking as they did because their sister had been defiled. "We could not do such a thing", they said, "as to give our sister to an uncircumcised man; that would be a disgrace for us. We will agree with you only on this condition, that you become like us by having every male among you circumcised . Then we will give you our daughters and take yours in marriage; we will settle among you and become one kindred people with you. But if you do not comply with our terms regarding circumcision, we will take our daughter and go away."

Their proposal seemed fair to Hamor and his son Shechem. The young man lost no time in acting in the matter, since he was deeply in love with Jacob's daughter. Moreover he was more highly respected than anyone else in his clan. So Hamor and his son Shechem went to their town council and thus presented the matter to their fellow townsmen: "These men are friendly toward us. Let them settle in the land and move about in it freely; there is ample room in the country for them. We can marry their daughters and give our daughters to them in marriage. But the men will agree to live with us and form one kindred people with us only on one condition, that every male among us be circumcised as they themselves are. Would not the livestock they have acquired- all their animals- then be ours? Let us, therefore, give in to them, so that they may settle among us.

All the able-bodied men of the town agreed with Hamor and his son Shechem, and all the males, including every able-bodied man in the community were circumcised. On the third day, while they were still in pain, Dinah's full brothers Simeon and Levi, two of Jacob's sons, took their swords, advanced agsinst the city without any trouble, and massacred all the males. After they had put Hamor and his son Shechem to the sword, they took Dinah from Shechem's house and left. The other sons of Jacob followed up the slaughter and sacked the city in reprisal for their sister Dinah's defilement. They seized their flocks, herds and asses, whatever was in the city and the country around. They carried off all their wealth, their women and their children, and took for loot whatever was in the houses.

Jacob said to Simeon and Levi: "You have brought trouble upon me by making me loathsome to the inhabitants of the land, the Canaanites and the Perizzites. I have so few men that, if this people unite against me and attack me, I and my family will be wiped out." But they retorted, Should our sister have been treated like a harlot.?"

Exodus 34:1-31

The Rape of Tamar

"Some time later the following incident occurred. David's son Absalom had a beautiful sister named Tamar, and David's son Amnon loved her. He was in such straits over his sister Tamar that be became sick; since she was a virgin. Amnon thought it impossible to carry out his designs toward her. Now Amnon had a friend named Jonadab, son of David's brother Shimeah, who was very clever. He asked him, "Prince, why are you so dejected morning after morning? Why not tell me?" So Amnon said to him, "I am in love with Tamar, my brother Absalom's sister." Then Jonadab replied, "Lie down on your bed and pretend to be sick. When your father comes to visit you, say to him 'Please let my sister come and encourage me to take food. If she prepares something appetizing in my presence, for me to see, I will eat it from her hand. So Amnon lay down and pretended to be sick. When the king came to visit him, Amnon said to the king, " Please let my sister Tamar come and prepare some fried cakes before my eyes, that I may take nourishment from her hand."

David then sent home a message to Tamar, "Please go to the house of your brother Amnon and prepare some nourishment for him." Tamar went to the house of her brother Amnon, who was in bed. Taking dough and kneading it, she twisted it into cakes before his eye's and fried the cakes. Then she took the pan and set it out before him. But Amnon would not eat; he said, "Have everyone leave me." When they had all left him, Amnon said to Tamar, "bring me nourishment into the bedroom, that I may have it from your hand." So Tamar picked up the cakes she had prepared and brought them to her brother in the Bedroom. But when she brought them to him to eat, he seized her and said to her, "Come!, Lie with me my sister!" But she answered him, "NO my brother! Do not shame me! This is an intolerable crime in Israel. Do not commit this insensate deed. Where would I take my shame? And you would be a discredited man in Israel. So please, speak to the king; he will not keep me from you."

Not heeding her plea, he overpowered her; he shamed her and had relations with her. Then Amnon conceived an intense hatred for her, which far surpassed the love he had had for her. "Get up and leave," he said to her. She replied, "No brother, because to drive me out would be far worse than the first injury you have done me." He would not listen to her, but called the youth who was his attendant and said, "Put her outside, away from me, and bar the door after her." Now she had a long tunic, for that is how maiden princesses dressed in olden days. When his attendant put her out and barred the day after her, Tamar put ashes on her head and tore the long tunic in which she was clothed. Then, putting her hands to her head, she went away crying loudly. Her brother Absalom said to her: Has your brother Amnon been with you? Be still now, my sister; he is your brother. Do not take this affair to heart." But Tamar remained grief-stricken and forlorn in the house of her brother Absalom. King David, who got word of the whole affair became very angry. He did not, however, spark the resentment of his son Amnon, whom he favored because he was his firstborn. Absalom, moreover, said nothing at all to Amnon, although he hated him for having shamed his sister Tamar.

2 Samuel 13:1-22

INCEST

Since Lot was afraid to stay in Zoar, he and his two daughters went up from Zoar and settled in the hill country, where he lived with his two daughters in a cave. The older one said to the younger: "Our father is getting old, and there is not a man on earth to unite with us as was the custom everywhere. Come let us ply our father with wine and then lie with him, that we may have offspring by our father." So that night they plied their father with wine, and the older one went in and lay with her father; but he was not aware of her lying down or getting up. Next day the older one said to the younger. "Last night it was I who lay with my father.. Let us ply him with wine again tonight, and then you go in and lie with him, that we may both have offspring by our father." So that night, too, they plied their father with wine , and then the younger one went in and lay with him; but again he was not aware of her lying down or getting up.

Thus both of Lot's daughters became pregnant by their father. The older one gave birth to a son who she named Moab, saying, "From my father." He is the ancestor of the Moabites of today. The younger one, too gave birth to a son,

and she named him Ammon, saying, "The son of my kin." He is the ancestor of the Ammonites of today.
Genesis 19:30-38

"None of you shall approach a close relative to have sexual intercourse with her. I am the LORD. You shall not disgrace your father by having intercourse with your mother. Besides, since she is your own mother, you shall not have intercourse with her. You shall not have intercourse with your father's wife, for that would be a disgrace to your father. You shall not have intercourse with your sister, your father's daughter or your mother's daughter, whether she was born in your own household or born elsewhere. You shall not have intercourse with your son's daughter or with your daughter's daughter, for that would be a disgrace to your own family. You shall not have intercourse with the daughter whom your father's wife bore to him, since she, too, is your sister. You shall not have intercourse with your father's sister, since she is your father's relative. You shall not have intercourse with your mother's sister, since she is your mother's relative. You shall not disgrace your father's brother by being intimate with his wife, since she, too, is your aunt. You shall not have intercourse with your daughter in law; she is your son's wife, and therefore you shall not disgrace her. You shall not have intercourse, with your brother's wife, for that would be a disgrace to your brother. You shall not have intercourse with a woman and also with her daughter, nor shall you marry and have intercourse with her son's daughter or her daughter's daughter; this would be shameful, because they are related to her. While your wife is still living you shall not marry her sister as her rival; for thus you would disgrace your first wife…
Leviticus 18:1-18

If a man disgraces his father by lying with his father's wife, both the man and his stepmother shall be put to death. They have forfeited their lives. If a man lies with his daughter-in-law, both of them shall be put to death; since they have committed an abhorrent deed, they have forfeited their lives. If a man marries a woman and her mother also, the man and the two women as well shall be burned to death for their shameful conduct, so that such shamefulness shall not be found among you.

Leviticus 20:11-12

If a man consummates marriage with his sister or his half sister, they shall be publicly cut off for their people for this shameful deed; the man shall pay the penalty for having intercourse with his own sister.

Leviticus 20:17

You shall not have intercourse with your mother's sister or your father's sister; whoever does so shall pay the penalty of incest. If a man disgraces his uncle by having intercourse with his uncle's wife, the man and his aunt shall pay the penalty by dying childless. If a man marries his brother's wife and thus disgraces his brother, they shall be childless because of this incest.

Leviticus 20: 19-21

Now Herod had arrested John, bound [him] and put him in prison on account of Herodias, the wife of his brother Philip, for John had said to him, "It is not lawful for you to have her." Although he wanted to kill him, he feared the people, for they regarded him as a prophet. But at a birthday celebration for Herod, the daughter of Herodias performed a dance before the guests and delighted Herod so much that he swore to give her whatever she might ask for. Prompted by her mother, she said, "Give me here on a platter the head of John the Baptist." The king was distressed, but because of his oaths and the guests who were present, he ordered that it be given, and he had John beheaded in the prison. His head was brought in on a platter and given to the girl, who took it to her mother. His disciples came and took away the corpse and buried him; and they went and told Jesus.

Matthew 14: 3-12

"Cursed be anyone who has relations with his father's wife, for he dishonors his father's bed!" And all the people shall answer, "Amen!"

Deuteronomy 27:20

"Cursed be anyone who has relations with his sister, whether his father's daughter or his mother's daughter!" And all the people shall answer, "Amen!"

Deuteronomy 27:22

"Cursed be anyone who has relations with his mother-in-law!' And all the people shall answer, "Amen!"

Deuteronomy 27:23

Incest, having sexual relations with a close relative was strictly prohibited in the bible. One reason is that sexual intimacy with a family member would destroy personal relations within the family. Jealousy, hurt, subterfuge, would all result. Penalties included death or being cut off from the community. Of the twelve curses mentioned in the bible three apply to incest. Sexual intercourse with a close relative often resulted in genetically damages offspring. When Lot's daughters plied him with wine an got him drunk and slept with him, they got pregnant and gave rise to the Moabite and Ammonites people who were oftencursed in the bible.

PROSTITUTION

"Everything is lawful to me" but not everything is beneficial. "Everything is lawful for me," but I will not let myself be dominated by anything. Food for the stomach and the stomach for food," but God will do away with both the one and the other. The body, however is not for immorality, but for the Lord, and the Lord is for the body; God raised the Lord and will also raise us by his power.

Do you not know that your bodies are members of Christ? Shall I then take Christ's members and make them the members of a prostitute? Of course not! [Or] do you not know that anyone who joins himself to a prostitute becomes one body with her? For "the two," it says "will become one flesh." But whoever is joined to the Lord becomes one spirit with him. Avoid immorality. Every other sin a person commits is outside the body, but the immoral person sins against his own body. Do you not know that your body is a temple of the holy spirit within you, whom you have from God, and that you are not your own? For you have been purchased at a price. Therefore glorify God in your body.

1 Corinthians 6:12-20

Give not yourself to harlots, lest you surrender your inheritance.

Sirach 9:6

Wine and women make the mind giddy, and the companion of harlots becomes reckless. He who lightly trusts in them has no sense, and he who strays after them sins against his own life. Rottenness and worms will possess him, for contumacious desire destroys its owner.

Sirach 19:2-4

He who loves wisdom makes his father glad, but he who consorts with harlots squanders his wealth.

Proverbs 29:3

A man who consorts with prostitutes is a fool. The prostitute's increasing demands for payment for sexual favors soon bankrupts the man, and this is the least damage that she causes. If he is caught is reputation is tarnished.

In an age of sexually transmitted diseases that resist treatment his health and life are also at risk. Many prostitutes have dies from HIV-AIDS as well as their clients. Penicillin resistant syphilis and antibiotic resistant gonorrhea are also possible causes of ill health and death.

In the parable of the prodigal son (Luke 15:11-32) the one son squanders his share of his father's inheritance on a life of dissipation with prostitutes. While he loses all of his material goods, he also destroys a relationship with his brother who is angry with him.

The worst thing about prostitution, however, is that one risks his very soul sharing the sexuality of the prostitute and uniting his body, a temple of God, with hers. Whoever has sex with a prostitute destroys God temple, his own body.

In ancient days temple prostitutes of foreign gods wore cords around their waist that were broken when they had ritual sex with the temple worshipers. Their temple duty was fulfilled when they had sex with members of the cult. Prostitution was then especially hated by followers of God as it implied they who were consorting with prostitutes.

Sex with prostitutes is essentially adultery or fornication as it is sex between two married people or one married and one single persons, or two single persons. As such it is not a relationship between two people who are married to each other. Those who commit adultery and fornication will not enter the kingdom of God. To consort with a prostitute therefore condemns one to hell.

Prostitution and its followers risk their lives and their souls then. They have poor judgment. The users of prostitutes become reckless.

One famous story from the Bible references Tamar and Judah. Judah saw a woman by the side of the road who was dressed like a harlot but who was really his daughter-in-law, Tamar. He had sex with her and got her pregnant. When told that his daughter in law Tamar had played the Harlot and become pregnant, Judah wanted her dead until he discovered that it was he himself who had impregnated Tamar. She gave birth to Perez and Zerah.

Harlots are also depicted in the book of Ezekiel. In Ezekiel 23:1-49 Israelite cities are depicted as prostitutes that act as harlots and forsake God, and are punished for their crimes. Again in Ezekiel 16:1-63 Jerusalem is pictured as woman who honored by God but plays the prostitute and is punished by him.

The book Hosea in the Bible describes a man who marries a prostitute and has children to her. The prostitute was symbolic of Israel and her idolatry and oppression of the poor. Hosea did not abandon his harlot wife and God did not abandon his love of idolatrous Israel.

A harlot also appears in the Book of Revelation. Revelation 17:1-18 describes a woman wearing scarlet and purple adorned with precious stones, pearls and gold. The woman is described as being named "Babylon the great, the mother of harlots and the abominations of the earth."

IMMORALITY

Blessed are they who wash their robes so as to have the right to the tree of life and enter the city through its gates. Outside are the dogs, the sorcerers, the unchaste, the murderers, the idol worshipers, and all who love and practice deceit.

Revelation 22:14-15

For if God did not spare the angels when they sinned, but condemned them to the chains of Tartarus and handed them over to be kept for judgment; and if he did not spare the ancient world, even though he preserved Noah, a herald for righteousness, toether with seven others, when he brought a flood upon the Godless world; and if he condemned the cities of Sodom and Gomorrah [to destruction], reducing them to ashes, making them an example for the godless [people] of what is coming; and if he rescued Lot, a righteous man oppressed by the licentious conduct of unprincipled people (for day after day that righteous man living among them was tormented at the lawless deeds that he saw and heard), then the Lord knows how to rescue the devout from trial and to keep the unrighteous under punishment for the day of judgment, and especially those who follow the flesh with its depraved desire and show contempt for lordship.

Bold and arrogant, they are not afraid to revile glorious beings, whereas angels, despite their superior strength and power, do not bring a reviling judgment against them from the Lord. But these people, like irrational animals born by nature for capture and destruction, revile things they do not understand, and in their destruction they will also be destroyed, suffering wrong as payment for wrongdoing. Thinking daytime revelry a delight, they are stains and defilements as they revel in their deceits while carousing with you. Their eyes are full of adultery and insatiable for sin. They seduce unstable people, and their hearts are trained in greed. Accursed children! Abandoning the straight road, they have gone astray, following the road of Balaam, the son of Bosor, who loved payment for wrongdoing, but he received a rebuke for his own crime: a mute beast spoke with a human voice and restrained the prophet's madness.

These people are waterless springs and mists driven by a gale; for them the gloom of empty darkness has been reserved. For, talking empty bombast, the seduce with licentious desires of the flesh those who have barely escaped from people who live in error. They promise them freedom, though they themselves are slave of corruption, for a person is a slave of whatever overcomes him. For if they, having escaped the defilements of the world through the knowledge of [our] Lord and savior Jesus Christ, again become entangled and overcome by them, their last condition is worse than their first. For it would have been better for them not to have known the way of righteousness than after knowing it to turn back from the holy commandment handed down to them. What is expressed in the true proverb has happened to them, "The dog returns to its own vomit" and "A bathed sow returns to wallowing in the mire."

2 Peter 2:4-22

Put to death, then, the parts of you that are earthly: immorality, impurity, passion, evil desire, and the greed that is idolatry. Because of these the wrath of God coming [upon the disobedient].

Colossians 3:5-6

Make no mistake: God is not mocked, for a person will reap only what he sows, because the one who sows for his flesh will reap corruption from the flesh, but the one who sows for the spirit will reap eternal life from the spirit.

Galatians6:7-8

I say then: live by the spirit and you will certainly not gratify the desire of the flesh. For the flesh has desires against the Spirit, and the Spirit against the flesh; these are opposed to each other, so that you may not do what you want. But is you are guided by the Spirit you are not under the law. Now the works of the flesh are obvious: immorality, impurity, licentiousness, idolatry, sorcery, hatreds, rivalry, jealousy, outbursts of fury, acts of selfishness, dissensions, factions occasions of envy, drinking bouts, orgies and the like. I warned you, as I warned you before, that those who do such things will not inherit the kingdom of God. In contrast, the fruit of the spirit is love, joy, peace, patience, kindness, generosity, faithfulness, gentleness, self-control. Against such there is no law. Now those who belong to Christ [Jesus] have crucified their flesh with its passions and desires.

Galatians 5:16-24

And do this because you know the time; it is the hour now for you to awake from sleep. For our salvation is nearer now then when we first believed; the night is advanced, the day is at hand. Let us throw off the works of darkness [and] put on the armor of light; let us conduct ourselves properly as in the day, not in orgies and drunkenness, not in promiscuity and licentiousness, not in rivalry and jealousy. But put on the Lord Jesus Christ, and make no provision for the desires of the flesh.

Romans 13:11-14

Hence, now there is no condemnation for those who are in Christ Jesus. For the law of the spirit of life in Christ Jesus has freed you from the law of sin and death. For the law, weakened by the flesh, was powerless to do, this God has done: by sending his own Son in the likeness of sinful flesh and for the sake of sin, he condemned sin in the flesh, so that the righteous decree of the law might be fulfilled in us, who live not according to the flesh but according to the spirit. For those who live according to the flesh are concerned with the things of the flesh, but those who live according to the spirit with the things of the spirit. The concern of the flesh is death, but the concern of the spirit is life and peace. For the concern of the flesh is hostility towards God; it does not submit to the law of God, nor can it; and those who are in the flesh cannot please God. But you are not in the flesh; on the contrary, you are in the spirit; if only the Spirit of God dwells in you. Whoever does not have the Spirit of Christ does not belong to him. But if Christ is in you, although the body is dead because of sin, the spirit is alive because of righteousness. If the spirit of the one who raised Jesus from the dead dwells in you, the one who raised Christ from the dead will give life to your mortal bodies also, through his Spirit that dwells in you. Consequently, brothers, we are not debtors to the flesh, to live according to the flesh. For if you live according to the flesh, you will die, but if by the spirit you put to death the deeds of the body, you will live.

Romans 8:1-13

So, I declare and testify in the Lord that you must no longer live as the Gentiles do, in the futility of their minds; darkened in understanding, alienated from the life of God because of their ignorance, because of their hardness of heart, they have become callous and have handed themselves over to licentiousness for the practice of every kind of impurity to excess. That is not how you learned Christ, assuming you have heard of him and were taught in him, as truth is in Jesus, that you should put away the old self of your former way of life, corrupted through deceitful desires, and be renewed in the spirit of your minds, and put on the new self, created in God's way in righteousness and holiness of truth.

Ephesians 4:17-24

So be imitators of God, as beloved children, and live in love, as Christ loved us and handed himself over for us as a sacrificial offering to God for a fragrant aroma. Immorality or any impurity or greed must not even be mentioned among you, as is fitting among holy ones, no obscenity or silly or suggestive talk, which is out of place, but instead thanksgiving. Be sure of this, that no immoral or impure or greedy person, that is, an idolater, has any inheritance in the kingdom of Christ and of God.

Ephesians 5:1-5

Where do the wars and where do the conflicts among you come from? Is it not from your passions that make war within your members? You covet but do not possess. You kill and envy but you cannot obtain; you fight and wage war. You do not possess because you do not ask. You ask but you do not receive, because you ask wrongly, to spend it on your passions. Adulterers!

James 4:1-4

Therefore since Christ suffered in the flesh, arm yourselves also with the same attitude(for whoever suffers in the flesh has broken with sin), so as not to spend what remains of one's life in the flesh on human desires, but on the will of God. For the time that has passed is sufficient for doing what the Gentiles like to do: living in debauchery, evil desires, drunkenness, orgies, carousing, and wanton idolatry. They are surprised that you do not plunge into the same swamp of profligacy, and they vilify you; but they will give an account to him who stands ready to judge the living and the dead. For this is why the gospel was preached even to the dead that, though condemned in the flesh in human estimation, they might live in the spirit in the estimation of God.

1 Peter 4:1-6

Prostitution is always associated with evil in the Bible and one is wise to avoid these women. They swallow up wealth, consume the body and the soul, and cause one to become reckless. Sexual relations that involve payment to women are no different from adultery and fornication. Sexual relations outside those of consecrated marriage between men and women and that are not disposed to the bearing of children are not sanctioned by the bible.

In ancient times to the present there existed another form of prostitution between men and boys, or boy prostitutes. The book of 1 Corinthians 6:9-10 also makes clear that those who engage in this type of prostitution will also not inherit the kingdom of God-that they will forfeit heaven. All the other dangers of prostitution to include death from disease, and dissipation of wealth also apply to these relationships. Prostitution in any form is prohibited to Catholics, and other Christians. Anyone who buys the services of the people is foolish.

I first found about the abortion holocaust my second year of medical school in the pathology lab at the Reddy Memorial Hospital in Montreal. From that time on my conscience led me to speak out against the practice. In the beginning I was not aware how many were performed. The violence and utter senselessness of destroying innocent human life drove me to anger and frustration. When I became aware of the number of abortions performed each year and the cumulative numbers of abortions I became extremely concerned. Abortion could be the end of a civilization. It was genocidal.

I was not effective. Every time I spoke out I targeted myself from pro-abortion members of society. They never spoke to me but only acted against me. I lost jobs, lost my career, and almost lost my life in opposing these people. I took me a while to realize, that for whatever reason they choose to destroy and kill unborn human life, they were not afraid to destroy or kill those who opposed their agenda. Those from Planned Parenthood, to Emily's list to NARAL, had and agenda and purpose they did not want stopped. Be it racial profiling, to rich/poor friction, to woman's rights fanatics, to foreign interests who might want the United States destroyed within, to the democratic party, the forces were strong and energized. There was also profit in destroying human life which should not be discounted although the economics of abortion is folly.

I as a lone individual did what I could to change the tide. I voted in Presidential and local elections to try to pick pro-life candidates and gave hard earned money to support them. I fielded candidates for office. I wrote the supreme court and protested the Roe v Wade decision and petitioned Presidents to pick pro-life judges. I picketed abortion clinics and tried to dissuade abortion doctors from their gory work. I attended life chains to show people graphically the horror of abortion. I supported pro-life groups that ran billboards and ads in papers. I myself ran ads in papers to show the societal and adverse effects of abortion and presented television shows doing the same. Most importantly I tried to give my time and money to pregnant women so that they could have their babies. When it was apparent the government insisted on abortion on demand in its judicial system and government policy I took the case directly to the people.

I did lose however. From 1973 to 2014 sixty million abortions were performed in the United States of America. One in every four pregnancies was aborted. All of these abortions were completed in the name of women's "choice" and "freedom". While I probably stopped only a few abortions I did give women real choice. They saw for themselves the graphic nature of the abortion procedures which led every time to a dead baby and not some "tissue. We ripped off the pretty picture of abortion to show exactly what it was- killing a innocent human baby.

It is impossible to bring back to life a dead baby however I also tried to heal some of the suffering and pain people feel after an abortion. It is important to soften some of the callousness women develop after an abortion if this nation and society is to survive. The women were referred for counseling, and confession. Priests for Life and Sisters of Life offered life healing advice.

I too am a mortal man, the same as all the rest, and a descendant of the first man formed of earth. And in my mother's womb I was molded into flesh in a ten month's period— body and blood, from the seed of man, and the pleasure that accompanies marriage. And I too, when born, inhaled the common air, and fell upon the kindred earth; wailing, I uttered that first sound common to all. In swaddling clothes and with constant care I was nurtured. For no king has any different origin or birth, but one is the entry into life for all; and in one same way they leave it.

Wisdom 7:1-6

Before I formed you in the womb I knew you, and before you were born I dedicated you, a prophet to the nations I appointed you.

Jeremiah 1:5

Because they ripped open expectant mothers in Gilead, while extending their territory, I will kindle a fire upon the wall of Rabbah, and it will devour her castles Amid clamor on the day of battle and stormwind in a time of tempest. Their king shall go into captivity, he and his princes with him, says the LORD.

Amos 1:13-15

Children

Sex with a child, in our culture defined as someone sixteen our younger, is a grievous assault on a person. Not only is there the chance of physical damage to a child but there is more definitely possible emotional damage. The child does not have the experience or strength to resist and is at the whims of the adult. Sex with a child is taboo in that it violates the rights and integrity of a child. Sex with children in families or incest is especially egregious in that it involves a violation of what should be complete trust between an adult and a child- a trust that the sexual purity of a child should not be violated.

In today's culture there is sexual trafficking of children to please the desires of adults. Children who experience this probably cannot enjoy sexual relations as adults in marriage or later life because their boundaries have been so distorted. As usual children may become pregnant or be exposed to sexually transmitted diseases to include HIV AIDS.

For an adult to have sex with a child implies grave psychosocial problems of the adult. This cannot excuse however abuse of children. When kidnapping was included the arrest penalty was death. Jesus identified causing a child to sin with drowning in the depths of the sea. Perhaps this penalty is not severe enough.

The boy prostitute or a boy child used for prostitution purposes may have been abandoned to hell. How much more due the penalty to those who have violated and used these children. Today there are societies that define themselves as molesters of children (NAMBLA for example). It is certainly thoughtful for civil authorities to do whatever they can to destroy such groups.

Sex with children implies a power relationship. The adult has power over the child. In the least it is an abuse of power and should be met with long term prison sentences.

"Whoever causes one of these little ones who believe in me to sin, it would be better for him to have a great millstone hung around his neck and to be drowned in the depth of the sea. Woe to the world because of things that cause sin! Such things must come, but woe to the one through whom they come! If your hand or foot causes you to sin, cut it off and throw it away. It is better for you to enter life maimed or crippled than with two hands or two feet be thrown into eternal fire. And if your eye causes you to sin, tear it out and throw it away. It is better for you to enter into life with one eye than with two eyes be thrown into fiery Gehenna.
Matthew 18:6-9

Sex with Animals

"You shall not have carnal relations with an animal, defiling yourself with it; nor shall a woman set herself in front of an animal to mate with it; such things are abhorrent"
Leviticus 18:23

"If a man has carnal relations with an animal, the man shall be put to death, and the animal shall be slain. If a woman goes up with any animal to mate with it, the woman and the animal shall be slain; let them both be put to death; their lives are forfeit.
Leviticus 20:15-16

"Cursed be anyone who has relations with any animal!" And all the people shall answer, "Amen!"
Deuteronomy 27:21